GOODLOW'S
GHOSTS

Tor books by T.M. Wright

GOODLOW'S GHOSTS

T. M. Wright

TOR
HORROR

A TOM DOHERTY ASSOCIATES BOOK
NEW YORK

GOODLOW'S GHOSTS

Copyright © 1993 by T. M. Wright

This book is printed on acid-free paper.

A Tor Book
Published by Tom Doherty Associates, Inc.
175 Fifth Avenue
New York, N.Y. 10010

Tor® is a registered trademark of Tom Doherty Associates, Inc.

Library of Congress Cataloging-in-Publication Data

Wright, T. M.,
    Goodlow's ghosts / T. M. Wright.
      p. cm.
    "A Tom Doherty Associates book."
    ISBN 0-312-85466-8
    I. Title.
    PS3573.R544G64   1993
    813'.54—dc20   92-36939
                                                        CIP

First Edition: January 1993

Printed in the United States of America

0 9 8 7 6 5 4 3 2 1

For Cindy, whose character Sam is.

GOODLOW'S
GHOSTS

RYERSON BIERGARTEN

When he was fifteen years old and had discovered his psychic abilities, Ryerson Biergarten was positive he'd gone crazy. He knew about people who "heard voices," or saw faces in the wallpaper, or woke night after night from the same awful dream. So, when that sort of thing started happening to him, he went to his mother and asked her advice. She was at the sink, peeling potatoes. The water ran while they talked, so Ryerson's memory of the conversation would always be colored by the white noise of the water running.

She wore a knee-length white dress. Her blond hair hung long down her back.

Ryerson said, "I see things, Mom." He shook his head in confusion. "I see things and they come true." He paused. "Or I find out later that they're true." He closed his eyes a moment and went on, "And sometimes I know what people are thinking. I can *hear* what they're thinking, Mom, just like they were talking to me."

"And you suppose that you're crazy because of all this?" his mother asked.

Ryerson sighed. "I don't know, Mom. I don't know." He sounded as if he were in misery.

His mother nodded. "Tell me what you see, Ryerson." She adjusted the water that was running onto the potatoes because the hot was running out.

Ryerson shoved his hands into his pockets. He was, in many ways, a typical sixties teenager growing up in the suburbs just outside Boston. He was something of a slob, a trait he never grew out of completely. He was fascinated by The Beatles and Herman's Hermits and The Rolling Stones. His school work suffered from his preoccupation with girls, basketball, and acne. So, when his mother looked at him with that bemused expression on her face, and said, "Tell me what you see, Ryerson," what *she* saw was an awkward, vaguely scared-looking young man whose brown corduroy pants were baggy and whose shirttails hung out, and who was beginning to sport what might have generously been called a mustache. At the same time, this archetypal teenage boy was suffering torments that few other teenagers suffered, and she knew it.

Ryerson said to her, "I see all kinds of things, Mom," and quickly added, "I saw that Charlie was going to get hit." Charlie was their dog. He'd been hit by a school bus a week earlier and was recuperating in the garage—he had a broken leg and a cracked pelvis.

"When?" Ryerson's mother asked, and finally shut the water off.

"The day before it happened," Ryerson answered.

She turned around from the sink and folded her arms over her chest. Then she sighed, sat at the kitchen table, and asked Ryerson to sit opposite her. He did.

"And what else?" she asked.

He was confused. "And what else?" he said. "Don't you want to hear about Charlie?"

"We both know about Charlie, Ryerson."

He looked at her for a long moment until it became clear what she was saying—they both knew about Charlie, then, so he could be lying, or, at least, fooling himself. He clasped his hands nervously on the table top. He didn't like being mistrusted by his own mother. He said, staring at his hands and pouting a little, "And I know that Dad and you are going to get a divorce. I can hear you thinking about it."

Her face froze.

After a half minute, Ryerson said, "Mom?" He read pain in her. He *felt* her pain and her heartache. "Gee, God, I'm sorry," he said.

His mother stood, looked appraisingly down at him and said, "Never let anyone tell you that what you have is a 'gift,' son. It isn't."

A month later, Ryerson's father moved out of the house.

Very early on, Ryerson had glimpses of what he became convinced was the world of the dead. These glimpses were at first swift, and horrific, and he was as much afraid of them as tantalized by them.

His first such encounter was on a bright winter morning when he was fifteen years old.

He had just awakened. A snow had fallen overnight, and the morning sun glinted gaily off the snow and into his bedroom window.

His world at that moment was bright, and cold, and cozy.

It changed in an instant. It became dark, hot, claustrophobic.

He was no longer in his bedroom. He was in a room whose walls were close. And he was no longer lying in his bed. He was standing. He thought that he could reach and touch the walls of this room.

He could see little. His sudden confusion and fear prevented him from noticing much—a light fixture overhead, a chair, some kind of couch nearby, visible as only a fat lump in the darkness.

He smelled salt air. Fish.

He thought of calling for his mother.

He heard, "No mothers here." It was followed by a soft chuckle. Then faces appeared out of the darkness. They were faces whose mouths hung open and whose eyes were wide and hollow with fear, loneliness, hunger. He thought they were like the faces of the drowned appearing from dark water.

He heard, "Oh, we have use for you here, boy."

He screamed.

Then, all at once, the room was gone, he was in his bedroom again, and his mother was standing over him, shaking him, pleading with him, "Ryerson, my God, what's wrong?"

He stared at her.

She told him, "You were calling to me. You sounded like the hounds of hell were after you."

He didn't remember calling to her. He shook his head. "I . . . I . . ." He could think of nothing coherent to say.

His mother said, "You are a poor, unlucky boy, Ryerson."

At the time, he didn't know what she meant.

But in years to come, her words would come back to him, and he would understand.

RYERSON AT 33

Ryerson H. Biergarten (his friends called him "Rye") had the body of a long-distance runner, a face that was invariably described as "sexy," "intriguing," or both, and he dressed in a way that the first of his two divorced wives called "poor man's preppy," in faded, no-name jeans, and corduroys, battered yellow or brown cardigan sweaters, argyle socks, penny loafers, and well-worn blue, beige or green button-down shirts. ("It's clear, Rye," his first wife had told him, "that you don't give a damn what you look like." He had readily agreed.) He had a full head of reddish brown hair, usually in need of cutting or combing, and his gray-green eyes almost always had a spark of humor in them. He had also, in the past few weeks, taken to carting around a snorting Boston bullterrier pup he'd named Creosote. He called the dog Creosote because he had found it in a smokehouse behind a two-hundred-year-old farmhouse in Vermont. Ryerson had been in the farmhouse looking for several of its previous tenants—a man in his nineties who did lots of cursing at odd hours, and a young woman of twenty or twenty-one who had a fetching smile and wonderful green eyes. She liked to lounge on a huge, Victorian-style sofa in the parlor and say suggestive things to the house's male visitors. Both of these previous tenants were dead. The man in his nineties had died 110 years earlier, according to the County Hall of Records, and the woman had died at her lover's hands early in the twentieth century. Her name had been Gwendolyn, and the man's name had been Mr. Barclay.

Ryerson did not go to the house convinced of anything. He was, by nature, a skeptical person and was ready to find any of a number of answers, the most likely being that the owners of the house had cooked the whole thing up to draw visitors in. The owners, a group of five area businessmen, charged two dollars a head for people to walk through what they called a "living piece of America's heritage." Ryerson believed firmly in the supernatural, and he believed just as firmly in its various and usually unpredictable effects on the world of the living. He also believed, perhaps even more firmly, in the potential for greed and ignobility inherent in everyone (including himself—though, at the age of thirty-three, he liked to think that he hadn't yet fallen to too much greed, or too much ignobility).

He talked to each of the five businessmen first. He asked them pointed questions about what they'd heard and seen, the same question several times, from different perspectives, trying to catch any of them in a lie. And when he was done, his own very well-developed sixth sense told him that there was a little bit of hoax, a little bit of truth, and a lot of colorful exaggeration involved in the whole thing. Whether there was anything actually supernatural happening at the house was a judgment he would put off until he'd been through it.

He went there on a Monday, the day the house was closed to visitors, and to his surprise—and without much effort—he found the two ghosts he'd been hired to find. It was late afternoon, the day was dismal and rainy, and the young woman, Gwendolyn, was in her usual place on the huge Victorian sofa in the parlor. She was, as Ryerson liked to say, "flickering"—her image waxed and waned like the light of a candle. Her suggestive words waxed and waned in the same way.

"Hi," she said when Ryerson walked into the room.

"Hi," he said.

"Would you"—her image waned; her words grew inaudible—"me?"

"I'm sorry," Ryerson said. He had stopped in the doorway. He didn't want to go any farther. The truth was, although he'd investigated several hundred "events," as he called them, he had never been able to push back the loud whisper of fear. He'd tried smiling, coughing, whistling, he'd tried thinking about Yogi Bear, had tried logic *(My God, this poor creature is lost, and I'm here to help it!),* but still the fear remained. No matter that Gwendolyn, when he could see her, was probably the most delightful and sensuous of all the ghosts he'd encountered; she was still a ghost, so she made his stomach flutter and started a hard knot of fear in his throat.

"I want you to take your pants off," Gwendolyn said, and faded once more.

When she reappeared—she was lounging with her legs up on the Victorian sofa, and was dressed in an extremely low-cut red floor-length gown—Ryerson asked, "What good would that do?"

This confused her. Her brow furrowed. She glanced down at the floor briefly. When she looked up, she was smiling happily, as if she'd discovered something that had been missing for a long time. She said, "Well, we could diddle with . . ." The rest of the sentence was inaudible, but Ryerson thought he understood the gist of it.

"How?" he asked.

She faded, returned, faded, returned, and swung her feet to the floor. Ryerson was a little troubled by the total silence that accompanied her movements. He'd encountered the phenomenon a lot, but it, too, was something he'd never grown used to.

"How what?" she asked at last.

"How could we diddle with each other?"

"You don't like me? You don't want to diddle with me?" This seemed to hurt her. "Aren't I attractive enough?"

"You're very attractive. You're wonderfully attractive," Ryerson told her. "But, I'm sorry, you're dead. Do you know that?"

"No," she said, without hesitation, and faded again, returned, faded. She was gone for a full minute. When she reappeared, she was standing on the opposite side of the room near a tall, narrow window, her profile to Ryerson. The window's sheer white curtains had been drawn, and the dismal light of the afternoon was giving her an especially gray and chalky look that, Ryerson thought, she hadn't had when she'd been on the sofa. It was a look that was at once frightening and sad, and his heart went out to her when he saw it. She was, after all, another human being—her form was a bit altered, it was true, and she had long ago left life behind her, but she was another human being, nonetheless (much more a human being, he thought, than the rotting shell that had once been her body, buried in the country cemetery ten miles south of the house). "No," she said again, and added, "I don't know that." She said it slowly, at a whisper, eyes lowered, hands clasped in front of her. "I don't know that," she repeated. "I can't be dead. I *feel!* I *hear!* I *want!* The dead don't have any of that."

Ryerson said, "You are proof that they do."

And she faded again, returned, faded, returned, faded. And, at last, was gone forever.

Ryerson found the ninety-year-old man, Mr. Barclay, in the cellar.

Mr. Barclay once had a workshop there, where he built clocks. His specialty had been cuckoo clocks fashioned from cherry wood indigenous to the area. But he was a lousy clockmaker. He made one stupid mistake after another, so he was constantly cursing at himself, which is how Ryerson was able to find him.

"Fucking fairy farts!" Ryerson heard, in a voice that was old and cracking.

"Hello!" Ryerson called down the cellar stairs.

"Donkey tits!" he heard.

"Who's there?" Ryerson called.

"Rancid rat cocks!"

"You're awfully creative!" Ryerson called.

"Shit, shit, shit!"

"Most of the time."

"Who's there?" called the aged voice.

"I'd like to help you," Ryerson called.

"Bite my bird!"

"Are you building clocks?" Ryerson was still at the top of the stairs; he had found, more than once, that it was easier to talk to a voice alone than to a voice and the image of a body. Besides, there were no lights in the cellar, and Ryerson was all but blind in the dark. He added, "Are you building cuckoo clocks?"

"Lousy turd!"

"I want to help you. Will you let me help you?"

"Shit, shit, shit!"

"My name is Ryerson. I'm one of the living." It was a standard line, one he'd developed, and he was proud of it. He had a doctorate in psychology from Duke University (though no one except his first wife called him "Doctor"), and he thought that it was often best to let "the others" come to their own conclusions about whether or not they were still among the living. The whole issue was incredibly complex. "The world of the supernatural," he had told his students at a short-lived night class in the paranormal at New York University, "is every bit as pluralistic and multi-faceted as our own. Indeed, it is sometimes very difficult to tell the difference between the two. Each 'event' and each participant in an 'event' must be treated as an individual phenomenon—"

"Eat my shorts!" called the voice in the cellar.

This surprised Ryerson; wasn't *Eat my shorts!* a fairly recent phrase? Maybe the old man was picking up on what visitors to the house had been saying or thinking.

"I'm one of the living," Ryerson called back, and thought that the whole thing was going badly.

"Eat my shorts anyway!" called the voice.

And so it went. Eventually Ryerson closed the cellar door and decided to try again on another day, which was his usual procedure, anyway. Rarely was he able to placate one of "the others" on the first try. The chances were good, at any rate, that the group of businessmen who owned the house was just as content to have the hauntings continue.

It was when he was about ready to get into his 1948 Ford station wagon—a car that he'd spent a considerable amount of time and money getting into working condition—that he got a quick mental image of four dark, cold walls and he felt a sense of urgency, fear, and hunger. He looked about, saw the stone smokehouse a good hundred feet behind the farmhouse, and there found Creosote, who was terribly weak and thin. Ryerson called one of the businessmen, explained that he wanted to come back, that there was "additional work to do," and then mentioned Creosote, whom at the time he referred to only as "a damned pathetic Boston bullterrier pup."

"Shit, keep it," said the businessman.

So he did.

REGARDING
SAM

ONE

What intrigued Sam Goodlow most about being dead was the way it felt in his toes and in the tips of his fingers. It felt heavy. It felt as if there were fishing sinkers attached. He had no trouble moving, though. His fingers and toes moved as freely as they ever had. He thought he might even be able to play the piano.

He couldn't remember if he had been able to play the piano when he was alive, but he didn't think that it mattered. Weren't the dead free to do whatever they wished? They could levitate, disappear, read minds, transform themselves into monsters, or play the piano, although such abilities might have been far beyond them in life.

Sam remembered his name. Sam Goodlow. He remembered his last mortal moments on earth, remembered flying high into the air above the Lincoln Town Car that had run him down. He remembered a grinning face in the front seat of the Town Car, too, and remembered thinking that there was no justice in the world because the beefy guy grinning at him from the driver's seat of the Town Car would probably get away with this murder. And he remembered that *justice* had little to do with anything that really mattered in the universe.

It was the first time he had ever thought about the universe. In life his thoughts had been more mundane. Breakfast, shaving, getting laid. He had gotten laid often, not because he was disarmingly attractive. He wasn't. Or because he was rich. He wasn't. But because he was charming. He had always been charming. When he was a young man, his mother, his aunts and his uncles had told him a thousand times that he was going to be a "real lady-killer" when he grew up because he was so charming.

He didn't remember being told that he'd be a lady-killer, and he didn't remember getting laid, either. He didn't remember if he had played the piano, or why the big guy in the Town car had run him down, or even what he—Sam Goodlow—looked like (so far, mirrors showed him only an elongated mist with hair), or what he had *been,* in life.

But he thought it would all come back to him in time.

He felt good, and it surprised him. He hadn't expected— flying ass-over-teacup above the Town Car—that he would feel *bad.* He had expected that he would feel *nothing.* Wasn't that what most people expected from death? *Nothing.* Not cold or hot or lukewarm. Not pain or comfort or joy. Nothing.

He liked feeling good, of course. But he was distrustful of it, too. He thought that it meant he was being prepared for heaven. He remembered stories about heaven and remembered thinking that it was not a place he would like to spend much time. An eternity in the company of saints and angels and "good people" would surely be a bore.

He felt as if he had eaten well and was very relaxed. He felt as if he had found exactly the right position for sleep.

Oddly, he felt wet, too.

* * *

He closed his eyes. He could still see the room he was in. This shocked him. Seeing through his eyelids was something he'd never been able to do in life. It was proof of his situation, proof that he was dead.

He screamed.

Nothing came out.

He opened his eyes.

The room lightened.

He closed his eyes. The room darkened, as if he were seeing through sunglasses.

He opened his eyes. The room lightened.

He closed his eyes. The room darkened. He saw nothing at all.

He smiled and decided that maybe he was alive, after all. It was possible.

He remembered water.

A telephone.

He shivered. *Someone is dancing on my grave,* he thought.

And he remembered that his father had died when he—Sam—was only three years old, although he didn't remember his father's face. Perhaps here, in this new existence, it would eventually come back to him.

He realized that he had to pee. This shocked him. Did ghosts have bowels, kidneys, bladders? Were tales of the supernatural littered with accounts of toilets flushing in empty bathrooms? Maybe. What did he know? In life, he'd never been much interested in the occult, so maybe the world *was* filled with supernaturally flushing toilets.

Or maybe the fact that he had to pee was further proof that he was, indeed, alive.

He glanced about. Bathroom? he wondered. He thought

he should know where the bathroom was. This place was so hauntingly familiar.

An open door to his left. He went through it.

It was a closet. There was a broom, a pail with mop, a dustpan, some old newspapers on a shelf. "Dammit!" he whispered. He couldn't pee in here.

He heard a door open. He craned his head out the doorway, looked.

A short woman with wavy, shoulder-length, strawberry blond hair entered the room.

Sam pulled his head back in and stopped breathing.

RYERSON AT 35

Ryerson Biergarten said to his two-year-old Boston bullterrier, Creosote, sniffing around a pair of Ryerson's argyle socks (its favorite chew toys, especially if Ryerson happened to be wearing them, as he was now), "It's *passion* you feel for my socks, isn't it?" He knew that this was true because, from time to time, he was able to read Creosote's mind—not in any directly translatable way (he wasn't able to carry on a conversation with the dog), but in a way that let him know the dog's moods and appetites. Ryerson understood that Creosote had a sock fetish. And it was not a fetish for just any kind of sock, only argyles. Dimly, Ryerson knew it was the patterns on argyle socks that got the dog worked up.

Passion interested Ryerson today because he had just been thrown over by a woman he had fallen in love with—a woman who, he'd felt sure, had fallen in love with him. Her very last words to him were, "Yes, I do love you, Rye. But for reasons I'd rather not share, I am going to call us

completed." Ryerson liked the phrase, but not the senti-
ment, and he certainly didn't like the emotion that had
vaulted from her head to his when she'd said it. It had told
him very clearly that their six-week love affair was over, and
that it was what she wanted (*had* wanted for some time).

He whispered, "Damn, I miss her."

And so, his thoughts meandered, Creosote had a sock
fetish, he—Ryerson—had a broken heart, and the world
still turned 'round.

Creosote got a good hold on Ryerson's left sock, planted
his feet firmly in the carpet, and tugged hard, wheezing and
growling obscenely at the same time.

Ryerson admonished him, face to face, finger wagging,
"You mustn't *do* that, Creosote. It's annoying, and it's
destructive. I *like* my socks. I don't want them turned into
dog drool." Creosote continued tugging on the sock. Ryerson grinned. He knew that Creosote was having a wonderful time.

Ryerson forced the dog's jaw open, so Creosote released
the sock. The dog looked momentarily put out, then, after
another wheeze and gurgle, curled up at Ryerson's feet.
Ryerson reached down and scratched the dog's neck. Creosote gurgled, snorted, and sneezed.

TWO

J enny Goodlow glanced sadly about her brother's empty office and sighed. "Sam," she whispered, "you were a world-class slob."

Yes, she heard, *I'm aware of it!* She thought for one chilling moment that Sam had actually said it. But then she realized that it had not been Sam's voice but her memory of his voice, her memory of the thousand times she had told him he was a slob, and the thousand times that he had come back with "Yes, I'm aware of it!"

She said, "I miss you, Sam."

I miss you, too.

"You were so much more than just a brother."

No, I was just a brother.

She had come to the office to collect Sam's important papers, his personal items, and to close the office up. His lease was done. He had to clear out, anyway, she told herself.

She sighed. "Oh, Sam, where did you go?" she whispered.

She got no answer.

The task of cleaning the office out had fallen to her because she knew that Sam would want no one else to do it, although he had had plenty of male friends—charming slobs usually did, Jenny thought—a half-dozen girlfriends, and a brother (he lived on the west coast and neither Jenny nor Sam had seen him in years). She and Sam were as close as a brother and sister can be (even though she was only his stepsister), and Jenny knew that he would have wanted no one else to do this.

Where do I begin? she wondered. "Right where you're standing," she answered herself.

She bent over to pick up a coffee-stained T-shirt. It had a photograph of one of the Three Stooges on it with the words "Just say" above, and "Moe" beneath. She smiled. She'd gotten Sam the shirt on his forty-first birthday, just a month earlier.

She stopped smiling abruptly.

The toilet was flushing.

The bathroom door opened.

Jenny, her mouth open in surprise, stared at the woman who walked out. It was Sam's most recent girlfriend, Rebecca Meechum. What in the hell was *she* doing here?

"You're not supposed to be here!" Jenny said.

The woman lurched. She was exiting the bathroom sideways and closing the door behind her, so she hadn't noticed Jenny. Her hand fluttered to her chest.

"Good Lord, you *scared* me!" she proclaimed.

"You're not supposed to be here!" Jenny repeated.

Rebecca let her hand fall. She was slender, dark-haired, large-eyed, and was usually full of a well-cultivated poise, mannerly and pleasant. It was all an act, Jenny knew. She had seen it in the woman's eyes from their first moments.

"I don't see why I'm not supposed to be here," Rebecca said, and came forward so she was standing obstinately on the opposite side of Sam's desk, which was littered with playing cards, a few errant Cheerios, rubber bands, and unpaid bills. There were also several large coffee mugs; one contained coffee which, because of the cream in it, had turned bright green with age.

Rebecca went on petulantly, hands on her hips now, "I have as much right to be here as you do."

Jenny shook her head. "No you don't. Sam's dead, so you have absolutely no right to be here."

Rebecca looked confused. "Nobody's proved that he's dead, Jenny. Besides, what's that got to do with it? I know he would have wanted me to take care of his stuff, so that's what I'm doing."

"Why in the hell would he have wanted you to do anything for him?" Jenny protested. She knew she sounded foolish. Sam had been smitten hard by this beautiful phony, as difficult as it was for Jenny to believe.

Rebecca smirked. "Apparently, you had a sick relationship with him, Jenny. Just because he was your *step*brother doesn't mean that it's not still *incest!*"

"You bitch!"

In the closet, Sam had figured out that it was *him* these two women were talking about. They seemed to know him quite well. One, the blond, was apparently related to him and the other was . . . someone else.

He thought of calling out to them. Would they be able to hear him? *He* could hear *them.*

Then he wondered if that would frighten them. He was supposed to be dead. Hell, he *was* dead—the blond had said as much. And whether he was or wasn't, the living simply weren't accustomed to talking to people they assumed were dead, so it was probably best to stay where he was.

Or was it? Wouldn't his sister like to know if he was dead or not?

He wasn't sure.

He was very confused.

"Shit!" he muttered.

"What was that?" Rebecca said.

Jenny glanced at the closet; the door was open. Inside, she saw little but darkness. "I don't know," she said. "It came from in there."

"He had mice," Rebecca offered.

"He had *a* mouse," Jenny corrected. "One little mouse, and he caught it and took it to the park and let it go."

Rebecca shook her head, though Jenny was still looking at the dark closet. Rebecca said, "Nobody has just one mouse. That's stupid. If you see one mouse, you've got to assume . . ." Her voice was trembling. "You've got to assume that there are lots of mice, dozens of mice, a whole family of mice."

Jenny said, "Mice don't curse."

"I didn't hear a curse," Rebecca said.

Jenny glanced quickly at her, then back at the closet. "I did." She said nothing for a moment, then she called, "Who's there? Who's in the closet?"

Silence.

"Dammit!" she whispered. She thought of stepping closer to the closet. She was a good ten feet from it and could see the forms of the mop and pail and broom in the darkness, but she needed a better angle.

"It was next door," Rebecca said.

"Shutup," Jenny said.

"Those people next door are very loud. I've heard them. It's a record producer's office, you know, and they play this awful music, this awful rap music, and they play it so loud you can hardly—"

"Shutup, dammit!"

Rebecca shut up.

Jenny took a step to her right, so she had a better angle on the open closet door. It wasn't enough. She took another step. "Go and turn on the light," she told Rebecca, meaning the overhead fluorescent. The only light in the room now was what filtered in through the tall, grimy windows from the gray overcast outside.

Rebecca went quickly to the light switch near the door and switched it on. The single overhead fluorescent tube flickered into life, casting a yellow, shadowless light that illuminated half of the interior of the large closet. "Who's in there?" Jenny called.

"No one's in there," Rebecca said. She had a better angle on the closet than Jenny, and she could see nothing but the mop and the broom and the pail. "It's empty. It was mice." She seemed pleased.

"Mice don't curse," Jenny said again.

"This one did," Rebecca said.

Sam's fingers and toes no longer felt heavy. This concerned him. He thought that it *meant* something, though he had no idea what. His fingers and toes, his entire body, felt . . . airy. Light and airy and weightless. He'd never felt like that before. He'd always felt big and clumsy. Now, he felt as if he could float.

He wasn't sure he liked that idea. In life—if life was indeed behind him—he had been able to float only in his dreams. If he were able to float, now, it would mean that all the physical laws he had grown to accept without question—all the physical laws he had grown to count on in his years of living on the earth—meant nothing. And if those physical laws meant nothing, perhaps everything else meant nothing, too. And that meant that he was in for a lot of surprises.

But still, if he was going to float, how would he accomplish it? Did he merely have to *will* it, *think* about it? Did he have to *say* something—"Float!" ... "Levitate!" ... "Fly!" Did he have to lift himself up somehow, flap his arms and flail about like a windmill to create the proper updrafts?

It was obvious to him that merely *believing* he could float didn't make it so.

He felt a cold breeze. It crept up from behind him, from the closet wall, and it covered him like water.

THREE

"You don't like me much, do you?" asked Rebecca Meechum.

Jenny Goodlow was surprised by the question. "I don't think I've been subtle about my feelings."

"No," said Rebecca, smirking, "subtlety does not appear to be one of your strong points." She turned and started for the door, looked back. "I'll do this much for you," she said magnanimously. "Since we have so much in common"— meaning Sam—"I'll give you the dubious honor of cleaning up this place." She gave Jenny a quick, smug grin. "And then, should there be a funeral, we'll grieve together, we'll trade stories about him, we'll weep—"

"Why don't you just get out!" Jenny interrupted.

Rebecca said nothing for a moment. Then, with a little nod and another smug grin, she left the office.

When Sam Goodlow turned his head in the closet to see where the cold breeze was coming from he saw this:

A dimly lighted attic cluttered with collectibles—lamps, couches, clocks, rugs. A dust-covered telephone from the flapper era.

Things were moving about on the attic floor. They were

small and they moved quickly. He tried to peer at them, but then the breeze was gone. He was once again standing in the dark closet.

He felt wet.

And he was convinced that he was alive.

Ryerson Biergarten always woke with a start, as if someone had slapped him across the face. He often wondered why he woke this way and the only theory that made sense to him was this: Throughout the night, psychic input built up in his head, like water behind a dam—input from the people in the houses around him, and from the animals around him, too, even from the birds that lived in the attic, and the squirrels that cavorted in the oak tree in front of his house, input from the tail end of a thousand bad dreams floating into the atmosphere above Boston (or wherever he happened to be)—until, at last, and always precisely six hours after he fell into sleep, the dam let go and flooded his head with garbage. That was the way he thought of it. Garbage. Because when he woke it all drifted off like so much mental flotsam and jetsam on the outgoing morning tide. And though he had tried often, he could read none of it—it was like trying to read a newspaper that's been turned into papier-mâché.

But this rainy morning he woke with a start, watched the garbage floating off on the morning tide, and he found that he could read a small bit of it, that he could pull from it the sense of something toxic, pervasive, and insidious.

One world encroaching upon another.

Creosote, asleep on the floor beside the bed, woke when Ryerson woke, turned his flat, gummy face up toward his master, as if asking what was troubling him so, and gurgled deep in his chest. Ryerson could say nothing to him, though. Ryerson was scared, he didn't know why, and for the first time in a very long time, he did not bound from the bed and launch himself into the shower (which usually chased all the garbage away completely).

This morning he lay still.

FOUR

Boston's Twelfth Precinct homicide captain was a short, thin, balding man whose name was William Willis. His friends called him Bill. Everyone else called him Captain Willis.

He said to Ryerson Biergarten, seated in front of his desk, "Let me tell you why I've asked you down here." He offered Ryerson a jelly bean from a decanter.

"Thanks," Ryerson said, picked two purple jelly beans from the decanter and popped them into his mouth.

Captain Willis took a handful of the jelly beans and laid them out on his desk. He arranged them in single file as he spoke: "Twelve days ago, a man disappeared. His name was Sam Goodlow. He was a private investigator who worked with us from time to time—like you do, though not, of course, in the same capacity." Willis grinned. On his thin, boyish face it looked apologetic. He said nothing for a few moments, as if waiting for some input from Ryerson, and when Ryerson said nothing, Willis continued, "We believe that Sam Goodlow was murdered, and since he's apparently someone you knew, I thought you might help us."

Ryerson shook his head. "I don't know him."

"You're sure?"

"I shouldn't be?"

"Your name was written in his appointment book." Willis opened a file folder on his desk, took out a sheet of paper, and handed it to Ryerson. It was a page from an appointment book, and it was dated two weeks earlier. These words were written on it: "Ryerson Biergarten? Sledge's 12:30?"

"Sledge's?" Ryerson asked.

"It's a restaurant on the south side."

Ryerson handed the piece of paper back. "I'm sorry, Bill, but this is absolutely meaningless to me." He hesitated. "And I notice that he has question marks after each notation. My guess is that he only planned on making an appointment with me and never did."

Willis looked incredulous. "So you've never met this guy?"

"Never."

Willis tucked the piece of paper back into the file folder. He took out an 8×10 color photograph and handed it across the desk. Ryerson took it, glanced at it. The photograph showed a man with a square, craggy face, a tangled mop of red hair, and large, gentle, and expressive eyes. The man was smiling; his teeth were crooked. Willis said, "That's our boy. Sam Goodlow."

Again Ryerson shook his head. "Bill, I'm sorry, but I really have not met him."

Willis looked disappointed. "Well then, maybe you can . . . divine something from his photograph."

"*Divine* something, Bill?" Ryerson was offended.

Willis shrugged. "Isn't that what you do? You get impulses from things, like photographs? Shit, Rye, you've done it before. Don't make me think that I called you down here for nothing."

Ryerson said, "I'm afraid that's precisely what you did,

Bill." He tapped the photograph with his finger. "This man and I have never met. If we have, then I don't remember it." He handed the photograph back.

"Okay then," Willis said. "Thanks, anyway. If you get some kind of . . . rush of enlightenment . . ."

Ryerson stood. "I'll call you."

What, Sam Goodlow wondered, had prevented him from showing his sister that he was *alive?*

Perhaps, he had wanted not to frighten her. She was apparently convinced that he was dead. She might have thought he was an imposter, someone who meant her harm.

Why were you hiding in the closet? she would have asked. And how would he have answered her? He would have had no answer. Why had he been hiding in the closet, indeed?

And if she had asked him to *prove* he was Sam Good-low—*Show me some ID,* for instance, or, *If you're really my brother, then you'll know my special nickname for you*—he would have been at a real loss because he had no ID and he remembered nothing beyond the fact that someone had run him down. Obviously, he had amnesia. He'd hit his head and now he remembered nothing. But getting his sister to believe *that* would have been tough. He didn't *look* like he'd been run over. He didn't *look* like he had amnesia.

What *did* he look like? he wondered.

Was there a mirror in this place?

He glanced about. Desk. Floor lamp. Red upholstered desk chair. Cot. Diploma on the far wall. No mirror. But he remembered looking in a mirror earlier. Where had he been?

He couldn't remember.

He sighed. What was this place? he wondered.

It seemed so hauntingly familiar. It sparked such a strong

feeling of déjà vu in him. Clearly he had once spent a lot of time here.

He moved across the room and read the name on what he had thought was a diploma. "Samuel Goodlow," he read. "Licensed Private Investigator. Temporary Permit, Boston Police Department." He stared blankly at the words for a few moments, as if they were merely spots on the paper. He read them again. And again.

Samuel Goodlow? he wondered. Was *he* Samuel Goodlow? Did people call him *Samuel? Sam?*

He remembered so very little. He remembered flying ass-over-teacup above the Lincoln Town Car that had run him down. He remembered landing on his stomach on the roadway. He remembered being hit again. Remembered pain.

A telephone.

Nothingness.

Nothingness.

He shivered. *Someone just danced on my grave!* he thought again.

His fingers and toes felt heavy. He raised his hand, studied it a moment. Was this Sam Goodlow's hand? Was this *his* hand? Was it attached to *his* wrist, *his* arm, *his* shoulder?

He felt very tired.

He thought that he could sleep for a long, long time.

Ryerson had a housekeeper and his name was Matthew Peters. Matthew had a Ph.D. in creative writing, but he had published only a few numbingly hard to understand short stories in literary reviews. He had a novel making the rounds of New York City publishers, but it was a bad novel, horribly overwritten, full of lousy imagery and fractured syntax, and once every week or ten days he got his manuscript back with a form rejection slip. Matthew secretly

suspected that it was a bad novel, but he dreamed of someday showing the world that his Ph.D. in creative writing
meant something, so he ignored the rejections. He told himself that the literary world simply wasn't ready for him.

He couldn't ignore his poverty, though, which was why
he had taken the job as housekeeper for Ryerson Biergarten.

He was a very good housekeeper. He loved to polish
things, clean things, dust, put things in order. *A place for
everything and everything in its place* was his motto. He was
neat and *tidy*. He was scrupulously clean-shaven and well-
coifed, and his polyester pants always had a knife-edge
crease.

He was also very bad at taking and relaying messages.

Two weeks earlier he had taken a message from Sam
Goodlow. "Important we talk, Mr. Biergarten. Matter of
identification. Meet me at Sledge's, 7:15 P.M. tonight."

Matthew had written the message verbatim on a small
notepad on a telephone table in the foyer, then, while cleaning, had put the notepad in the drawer of the telephone
table because the yellow pad clashed with the dark wood of
the table.

Two weeks later, the notepad still rested in the desk
drawer.

The woman looked to be in her early sixties. She was well-
dressed, in a gray business suit, and her smile was spontane-
ous and businesslike at the same time. She carried a gray
umbrella, and it dripped on the carpet.

The woman was attractive, and the bank officer who
offered her a seat in front of his desk thought, not for the
first time, that one day he would find the courage to ask her
out to dinner.

"Good morning, Mrs. McCartle," he said. "You're looking very well."

"Thank you, Roger," the woman said, still smiling. The bank officer's name was Roger Fagen. "How is your wife feeling?"

Roger conjured up a look of concern. "The doctors think that she'll be okay, as long as she gets the rest she needs. But you know Margaret—always on the go."

"A woman devoted to her work, Roger. You should be proud."

Roger nodded vaguely in an attempt to get off the subject of his wife. He started to speak—*Actually, Margaret and I have been kind of on the outs, lately* was on his mind—but the woman said, "Let me tell you why I've come in today, Roger."

"Certainly." He conjured up a look of staid professionalism. "What can I do for you?"

"I'd like to transfer some money, again, from my account to an account in my sister's name, at another bank. That's not a problem, is it?"

"No problem at all. How much did you want to transfer?"

"I was thinking of one hundred thousand today, Roger."

He looked flustered. This was not the first such request the woman had made lately. In the past two weeks, she had transferred large sums to other accounts at least a half-dozen times. "One hundred thousand," Roger said, and smiled unsteadily. "Certainly, Mrs. McCartle. If you could wait here a moment, I'll get the ball rolling. It will take a few minutes, as you know."

"Of course, Roger," she said.

REGARDING RYE

FIVE

It was around noon, the following day, and a young couple named Stevie and Jack Lutz were strolling on a path behind their home in a rural area west of Boston. The path led to a stand of deciduous trees, circled back through several acres of fields, and ended in the Lutzes' side yard.

To a disinterested observer, Stevie and Jack might have appeared to be a happy couple, much in love. Today, as usual, they strolled hand in hand and talked often.

Stevie said, "I liked last night."

Jack said, "Me, too."

"You're very adventurous, aren't you?" Stevie said.

"I boldly go where no man has gone before," Jack said, and grinned.

"You and Magellan," Stevie said.

They had had this same conversation a hundred times during their relationship. Jack found it titillating. Stevie did not, although she had never shared this fact with him. She wanted to keep him happy. He didn't know it, but for a while now she had been looking for a way out of the marriage. No way seemed clear. Their relationship had lasted since they were both young teenagers and she thought that

that meant they were destined to be together for life. There was little, if anything, that she could do about it. So, keeping him happy—at least with himself—was what concerned her most. If he was happy, he might eventually figure out how to make *her* happy—if it mattered to him, and she wasn't at all sure that it did.

They had moved into their rural house quite recently and this was only their second walk through the woods and fields. They weren't familiar yet with the area's topography or landmarks. On their first walk a week earlier, they had noticed an old fence with several POSTED signs attached; they had also come across the gray and cheerless remains of a treehouse, the rusted hulk of an old car, and a huge oak tree split down the middle. But they could not recall now where any of these things were, precisely.

Jack let go of Stevie's hand and grabbed her rear end. They walked this way for a couple of yards and then his hand rose so it was around her waist. Stevie thought, for the thousandth time, that if all their relationship consisted of was sex, then maybe it would be all right.

Jack nodded at what looked like a roof off the path a dozen yards. From where they stood, they could see only the roof; any structure beneath was hidden by tall weeds and bushes.

They were not far from the stand of woods. Their house was well behind them, beyond a shallow rise, and the roof that Jack had nodded at was small and brown. He said that it was probably the roof of a hunter's cabin, and Stevie told him that she did not like the idea of hunters being in the area. Jack said that hunters were a fact of life in the country and she had better get used to it.

"Should we go and see what it is?" Stevie asked.

Jack shrugged and said there was no pressing need to do

that, but if she really wanted to, then it was not far out of their way. He felt very magnanimous allowing her this little detour from their scheduled route.

Stevie said, "Out of our way? I didn't realize that we actually had a destination, Jack."

"Well, I guess we don't," Jack said.

"Good," Stevie said, and started off the path. Jack followed after a few seconds, letting her lead by a couple of yards. He did not much like being in tall grass. He supposed that there was poison ivy, that there were insects and spiders.

After a few moments, Stevie stopped walking. They were not much closer to their destination; still, only the small brown roof was visible.

Jack stopped walking.

Stevie looked at him. "Do you smell that?" she asked.

Jack sniffed the air. He shrugged. "I don't know." His sense of smell was not as good as hers. He sniffed again. He shook his head. "I don't smell anything."

Stevie said, "Salty air. Water. A beach. It smells like a beach, Jack."

"You mean, like fish? I don't smell fish." He crinkled his nose at the very thought of smelling fish out here.

"I do," Stevie said. "It smells like the ocean." She smiled. She loved the ocean. She turned, started walking.

"Stevie, why don't we just let it alone," Jack called to her.

She stopped and looked back at him. "I don't want to leave it alone, Jack." She started forward again. Suddenly, she was feeling very independent, and very bold. She didn't know where the feeling was coming from, but she liked it.

"Keep in mind," Jack called, "that this is not even our property."

"Stiffneck," she called back, without turning to look at him.

"Stiffneck? I'm not a stiffneck!"

"Be as adventurous out here as you are in bed," she called.

"What?" he called back, because he hadn't heard what she'd said, and he realized with a little tremor of annoyance that she was all but lost in the tall grasses. "Wait up," he hollered.

He got no reply.

"Stevie?"

"C'mon," he heard.

The tall grasses hid her completely now.

"I can't see you," Jack called. "Where are you?"

"Here," he heard.

"Stevie, dammit, I don't like this." He hadn't moved since she'd told him she could smell the ocean. "Stevie, why don't we just forget this? It's not important." He glanced at the gray overcast that seemed to have come in in the last few minutes. "Stevie, I think it's going to rain again."

She reappeared from the tall grasses. To his surprise, she was only a few yards off. She looked peeved. "There's nothing here that'll bite you, Jack. Don't be such a baby. Don't be such a stiffneck."

He looked at her. He thought that there was something different about her, though he wasn't at all sure what. He said, "Are you all right?"

She looked more peeved. "Jack, if you don't come in here now, I'll see to it that something *does* bite you."

It was a joke, he thought, although he wouldn't have been able to tell by the angry look on her face.

"Okay," he said, "I'm coming." He started after her.

She smiled, turned away from him again, and disappeared into the tall grasses.

"Dammit, Stevie," he called, "will you *please* stay where I can see you?"

"I can't," he heard.

He stopped walking. "What do you mean you can't?" he called.

"I can't," he heard again.

He was getting very annoyed. He supposed that she might be playing some stupid, childish game with him. Heaven knew that her emotional age had yet to catch up with her chronological age. "Stevie," he called, "let's just keep walking on the path, all right. This really isn't necessary. It's someone else's property."

He heard her voice but could make out no individual words.

He sighed, whispered a curse, and pushed through the tall grasses toward where he had last seen her.

"Stevie, for Christ's sake!" he called.

And, in reply, he heard her voice again, though it was still unintelligible.

Then, what he had assumed was a hunter's cabin was before him. It had no windows. It was made of weathered gray wood, like barnwood, and appeared to be little more than ten or twelve feet wide on each side.

Stevie stood in the doorway. She smiled at him as if she'd been playing a joke. "You should see this place, Jack," she said with enthusiasm.

Then she turned and went inside.

"Dammit to hell!" Jack whispered, went up to the door, which was closed, hesitated, called to Stevie again and, getting no reply, pushed the door open and went inside.

The gray daylight did not easily penetrate the small structure's interior. Jack could see his wife, but she looked amorphous, tentative, and he wasn't sure that it was *she* he was looking at.

He said, "Stevie?"

"Isn't it wonderful, Jack?" he heard. Her voice sounded oddly distant.

"Isn't *what* wonderful?" Jack said. The room appeared to be unfurnished, except for a large overstuffed chair near Stevie; the chair was little more than a beige lump in the near-darkness. Jack said, "Why don't we just get out of here—"

"You can leave," Stevie cut in.

He laughed quickly.

"It's not a joke," she said.

He took a step closer to her. His eyes hadn't adjusted to the dim light yet and she was still hard to see. "Why would you want to stay in here by yourself, darling?" he asked.

"You call me *darling* when you're being parental," she said.

He smiled. "I become parental when you act like a child."

"Asshole!"

He bristled. "I do not like you to use such language, Stevie!" He glanced about. Why hadn't his eyes adjusted to the darkness? he wondered. It was as if this place . . . *stole* the light. "And I don't much like it here," he went on. He held his hand out to her. "C'mon, let's just continue our walk. You can make us both some tea when we get home."

"Make your own goddamned tea. I'm staying, Jack!" Her words were clipped, harsh.

He sighed again. "You're making me very annoyed, Stevie. I'm sure you don't want me to become annoyed."

"Then you can leave," she said.

"I'm not leaving without you."

"Then you'd better stay."

He let his hand drop. "For what?" he asked.

"For the hell of it," she answered, and laughed quickly.

He remained quiet a few seconds, then he said, "Is this some kind of stupid, childish game you're playing, Stevie?"

"I don't think so."

"Then can you tell me what the hell you're doing?"

She came forward. She stopped very close to him. He could see her face clearly, now.

He didn't recognize it. The features were the same—round blue eyes, small nose, full mouth, high cheekbones—but he knew that this woman standing before him was not his wife. This woman even had a different smell. She smelled musty.

He backed up a step.

"Who . . . are you?" he stammered.

The woman shrugged. She looked suddenly confused, uncomfortable. She said nothing.

He saw faces behind her in the darkness. He saw hands working, mouths grinning as if at the prospect of hunger being satisfied. "What in the name of God . . . ," he whispered.

He glanced quickly at the open door behind him, then at the woman again. She had backed away from him and was once more in shadow.

The other faces were gone, the hands reaching were gone.

"Where is my wife?" Jack pleaded.

He saw the form in the shadows move slightly and he guessed that she had shrugged again.

"Goddammit, *where* is my wife?"

The room was empty.

SIX

The headline on the front page of the *Enquirer* at Hearst's A&P, two blocks from Ryerson's town house on Market Street, read:

BIGFOOT GIVES BIRTH TO ELVIS'S BABY ON BOARD UFO

Ryerson chuckled when he read the headline. The chuckle quickly became a belly laugh, two belly laughs, three, until it was continuous.

He couldn't stop laughing. People ahead of him at the checkout stared at him, and people behind stared at him, but he couldn't see them through his laughter.

"What's so funny?" asked a woman in front of him.

He nodded toward the *Enquirer*. "That!" he managed.

BIGFOOT GIVES BIRTH TO ELVIS'S BABY ON BOARD UFO, she read.

"That's not funny," the woman said. "That's sick!"

"What's sick?" a man behind Ryerson asked.

"This headline," the woman said. "They're always saying these awful things about Elvis, and I wish they wouldn't. Now they're saying that he had sex with Bigfoot, and Elvis simply wouldn't *do* that. It's sick to even suggest it!"

"Bigfoot Gives Birth to Elvis's Baby On Board UFO," read the man behind Ryerson. He looked puzzled; Ryerson continued laughing. The man said to himself, "But that's not possible. UFO's aren't real."

A young woman behind him said, "It's *Bigfoot* that isn't real. *UFO's* are real. I've seen them."

Someone else said, "If it wasn't true, then they couldn't print it."

"They might have exaggerated," observed someone else. "You know, maybe this Bigfoot baby just *looked* like Elvis, so they assumed—"

Ryerson, chuckling now, bagged his own groceries as they were rung up, and left the store.

On the south side of Boston, in a bar called Sid's, a man named Bernie was coming on to a woman who told him her name was Bernice. Bernie exclaimed that the similarity of their names was a wonderful coincidence, that it was probably fate that they'd met, and when Bernice responded with only an "Uh-huh," he got onto another subject.

"I don't do this a lot," he said. "Drink in the middle of the day, I mean."

Bernice glanced at him. She had black, shoulder-length hair, was thin, large busted, and wore a green silk-look dress that was hiked up to midthigh. "Just needed to wet your whistle, huh?" she said, and sipped her white wine. Other than the bartender, who was paying them no attention, she and Bernie were the only people in the small, dimly lit bar.

Bernie nodded. "Yeah, wet my whistle. And you?"

Bernice shook her head. "I come in here every day. I stay here all day sometimes."

"What, drinkin' that stuff?" Bernie said derisively, and

nodded at the white wine. He was tall, stocky, thick necked, and his face was flushed from high blood pressure and too much alcohol. His eyes were small and muddy.

Bernice shrugged. "I get sick from booze."

Sid's was on the first floor of an apartment building that had seen its last regular tenant move out a decade before. The building was a big, square, red brick structure. Grinning cement gargoyles perched on the four roof edges, embossed, horn-blowing cement cherubs hovered under each of the two hundred windows, and bunches of cement grapes had been stuck over each window. The building was a monument to mid-Victorian bad taste.

Bernie said to Bernice, "Listen, I don't believe in foolin' around, you know. Why don't we go somewhere and screw each other till we drop." Bernie had used this line on a number of women. He thought it was direct and honest.

Bernice said, frowning, "You think I'm a whore? I'm not. I come in here to drink wine." She tugged the hem of her green silk-look dress to below her knees.

Bernie asked, "Did I say anything about *paying* you? All I said was why don't we go somewheres and get it on. I know you're not a whore."

Bernice said, "It ain't the middle of the day, anyway. It's supper time." She grinned oddly, which made Bernie uneasy, and finished, "And I'm very hungry."

"We'll eat first," Bernie said.

"I know just the place," Bernice said, got off her stool, took his hand, and led him to a stairway at the back of the bar.

"Up there?" he asked. He didn't want to go up the stairs. It was dark and the odor of mildew wafted down to him.

"Sure," Bernice answered, and surreptitiously rubbed her

breasts against his arm. "I live up there. I got an apartment. We'll have something to eat." She smiled playfully.

Bernie looked at her. She wasn't particularly pretty. Her nose was big and her eyes were a little crooked, her skin had a sad gray cast, and she looked tired. But her breasts were large, and this was what had interested him in the first place.

"You go ahead of me," he said, and she nodded, took his hand, and led him up the stairs.

Sam Goodlow hated doctors. He had no regular doctor and hadn't had a checkup in over a decade. He secretly supposed that there were many things wrong with him. High cholesterol, high blood pressure, and low stamina were chief among his worries, so he had lately been eating more chicken and less pork and crabmeat (to combat his supposed high cholesterol); he had been trying very hard to keep his emotions from bubbling over (because of his supposed high blood pressure); and he avoided doing anything that required too much effort. Hill climbing was out. Marathons were out. Kama Sutra–type sexual athletics were out.

He also slept as much as he could. He liked to sleep because his dreams were vivid and colorful and he often looked forward to them.

When he woke this morning, however, he thought that he had not dreamed at all. This disappointed him.

Stress, he decided, had deprived him of his dreams. He'd been under lots of stress lately. This new job gave him stress. The new *client* gave him stress—she'd stress anyone. Christ, she'd stress a dead man.

His phone rang. He looked at it. It was across the room, on his desk. "Shit!" he muttered. He didn't want to deal with anyone before he'd had his coffee.

The phone rang once more. He cursed again, got up from his cot, crossed the room, put his hand on the receiver.

The phone lay silent.

Whoever had been calling had let the phone ring only two times. "Asshole," he muttered.

He looked at his cot. He was still tired. He thought that he had never been so tired.

Bernice led Bernie down a wide, dimly lit hallway with very high ceilings. The woodwork was dark and had ornate leaf-motif scrollwork in it. Light in the hallway was provided by bare bulbs attached to what had once been gaslights.

Bernie and Bernice were on the third floor. Bernie was huffing and puffing from his climb up the stairs, and his chest hurt.

"We got far to go?" he asked Bernice, who still had hold of his hand.

She answered, without looking at him, "Not far. Down at the end of the hall."

"End of the hall," he echoed, and hoped he wouldn't collapse before they got there.

"You'll be all right," she told him. "I'll give you some dinner, then we'll screw."

They arrived at her apartment. She reached around him and pushed the door open, gestured, said, "Well, c'mon."

He nodded. His chest still hurt. Alarmingly, his left arm hurt, too. He hesitated. Her apartment was pitch dark. "Turn the light on," he said, and glanced at her.

"Silly," she said, gave him a pouting sort of smile, reached around the doorway, and flicked the light switch. An overhead light came on.

He looked inside. The apartment was bare.

"You live here?" he asked incredulously, his gaze on the room.

"After a fashion," she said behind him.

"But there ain't no furniture."

"Don't need no furniture," she said.

He glanced at her. She was grinning from ear to ear. It was a hideous grin against the sad gray mask of her face because her teeth were startling white and her lips were beet red. He hadn't noticed this before. He asked her, "You all right?"

"I'm fine," she whispered.

He looked away, into the apartment again. "What do you sleep on?" he asked nervously.

"Nothin'," she answered. "I don't sleep."

He glanced at her again. She was still grinning, but it wasn't as broad as it had been a moment earlier, and her teeth were not as glaringly white, her lips not as bright red. She looked more human. "Only joking," she said. "Go on inside. Please." She was pleading with him.

He shook his head. "No. I don't like this. It's weird. *You're* weird."

Her grin slipped. "You *have* to go in!" she exclaimed. "If you don't go in, we can't fuck. Please, Jack."

Bernie said, "Jack? My name's not Jack." Then he shook his head once, and again. The gesture became continuous, disbelieving.

Because her lips were again beet red, and her skin was gray, and her grin was growing impossibly wide.

He turned and ran from her as fast as his fat legs would carry him down the wide, dark hallway.

"Yes, Mrs. McCartle," said the real-estate man, smiling into the telephone. "I'm absolutely positive that your home would sell very quickly. As you know, there have already been several offers, but since you were unwilling—"

"That is the past, Ernest." The real-estate man's name was Ernest Anders. "Actually, I'm planning a move abroad, possibly a permanent one, and of course would have no need of this house."

"Of course."

"I would be selling everything, I think. House and furnishings together."

"Really?" He was smiling again. "Mrs. McCartle, that makes the property very valuable indeed."

"I'm aware of that, Ernest."

"And might I ask your time frame for this move abroad?"

"Within the month. Possibly sooner."

"That's very quick. I'll have to come out and do an inspection and appraisal right away."

Silence. Then, "No, Ernest. That won't be necessary. If I'm not mistaken, you inspected and appraised barely five years ago. I don't think the house has degenerated appreciably since then."

"Certainly, Mrs. McCartle. However, the buyer's bank is going to insist on an inspection. I'm sure you're aware of that."

Silence again. Then, "Ernest, perhaps I'll have to get back to you on this. It occurs to me that there are other matters to attend to before I can seriously discuss a sale of this property."

"I understand."

"I'm sure you do. I'll be in touch."

SEVEN

M y name is Jenny Goodlow," said the young woman at Ryerson's front door. She extended her hand; Ryerson shook it and invited her into the town house. She went in.

"We haven't met, have we?" Ryerson asked. The name Goodlow seemed familiar to him. He nodded and, before she could answer, went on, "Yes. Your brother's name is Sam, isn't it?" He had remembered the photograph that Bill Willis had shown him.

Jenny Goodlow said, "Yes," and looked confused. "But I thought that you and Sam had already met."

Ryerson sighed. "You're not the only one who thinks that." He gestured toward the living room. "Let's talk."

They went into the living room. Ryerson asked if she'd like some coffee; she said no and sat in a club chair near the window. She looked suddenly confused. "You *are* Ryerson Biergarten, aren't you?"

Ryerson nodded. "The only one in Boston." He was standing near her, at the window. There was another club chair close by and he sat in it.

Jenny Goodlow smiled a little, obviously embarrassed. "It's just that Sam talked about you once or twice and I assumed that you and he were friends."

Creosote appeared in the doorway that led to the dining room, regarded Jenny Goodlow with suspicion a moment, apparently decided that she wasn't a threat, and went and sat at Ryerson's feet. Ryerson reached down and scratched the dog's head. Creosote gurgled, wheezed. "Asthma," Ryerson said. "It's a fault of the breed."

Jenny Goodlow nodded vaguely and said, "My brother is missing, Mr. Biergarten."

"Call me Ryerson. Please."

She nodded again. She seemed very ill at ease and Ryerson cast futilely about in his head for ways to make her more comfortable. He quickly resigned himself to the fact that this was not a situation that could be made comfortable, so he chose simply to let her talk.

She shrugged. "If you didn't know him, I guess there's really no reason for me to be here, is there?" This seemed to be a prelude to getting out of the chair and leaving the house, but she merely looked questioningly at Ryerson, as if on the verge of speech, and stayed put.

Ryerson said, "I know that your brother's missing, Miss Goodlow. The police told me. They thought I could help—"

"You've helped them before, isn't that right?"

Ryerson nodded. "On a number of occasions, yes."

"And what did you tell them this time?"

Ryerson changed position in the chair but did not answer at once. Creosote glanced up at him, gurgled, lay down, and put his face on his paws, clearly aware that his master was becoming uncomfortable.

Ryerson said, "Well, they assumed, as you did, that I knew your brother. They found my name in one of his appointment books—"

"And you told them that you didn't know him?"

Ryerson changed positions in the chair again. She was *grilling* him, he realized. She was trying to trap him in a lie. He tried to read her, but her face was impassive, her large green eyes betrayed nothing. Ryerson said, "Clearly you believe that I *did* know him, Miss Goodlow, and clearly you believe that I'm keeping something from you. Isn't that right?"

"I knew my brother very well, Mr. Biergarten," she answered. "I trusted him. He spoke of you, and I assumed that he knew you." She paused. "I *don't* know you, however, do I?"

Ryerson sighed. "Why would I lie?"

"How can I answer that, Mr. Biergarten? If I don't know you, then I couldn't possibly judge your motivations—"

"I never met your brother," Ryerson cut in. There was a sharp edge of impatience in his tone. "The police showed me his photograph, and that was the first time I'd ever seen him. He'd written my name in his appointment book." A pause. *"I* can't help what he writes in his appointment book, can I?" He closed his eyes; he disliked becoming angry.

"I'm sorry, Mr. Biergarten—"

He heard her stand up. He opened his eyes, gestured for her to sit down again. "No. I'm sorry. Please stay. Perhaps I can . . . help you." He made the offer primarily because he wished to apologize.

She shook her head and looked icily at him. "No. If you didn't know Sam, then you can't help me." And with that, she left the house.

Sam Goodlow did not want to sleep but thought he had no choice. His body wouldn't let him stay awake. This concerned him. He thought it was proof that something was not right, and—as much as he disliked the idea—he supposed that he had better find a doctor before long and have a checkup.

He was sitting on the edge of his cot, and his hands were cupping the sides of the skinny mattress.

He glanced at the pillow. It looked inviting. It was fluffed and white, as if no one had used it. He whispered, "Too much sleep. Too much sleep." Life was passing him by. What was he accomplishing flat on his back, dead to the world? And why did he always feel *wet?* He glanced at himself. He didn't *look* wet.

With effort, he stood, glanced longingly at the pillow again, then crossed to his desk. He stood behind it, leaned forward, with his hands flat on the desk and his arms straight.

He didn't recognize his hands. They were too . . . large? Too wide? Too pale? He didn't know. He wasn't sure. He was sure that they weren't his hands.

He shook his head quickly. What in hell was he thinking? Of course these were his hands. Whose hands were they if they weren't his?

He thought that they penetrated the desk. A quarter of an inch. Less. They were a part of the blond wood, one with the blond wood.

He straightened, suddenly frightened.

He needed to sleep.

He looked longingly again at the cot across the room.

At times, Rebecca Meechum thought she almost regretted what she had done to Sam Goodlow. If it hadn't been so *easy* to do it to him, if he hadn't *invited* it, if he hadn't let his guard down and become so vulnerable, then perhaps she would have regretted what she'd done. But people, like him, who were foolish enough to let themselves be used by people like her, deserved whatever they got. What was the phrase?—*There's a sucker born every minute.* Sam was a sucker, and she was going to be ten thousand dollars richer because of it.

She didn't spend long thinking about what might have become of him. If he was dead, then it was too bad. But, hell, everyone died. Did it really matter when, or how?

She looked at the large manilla envelope on her kitchen table. It was sealed, and she had been warned not to open it. She wished the woman would come and pick it up. Having it around was too much temptation. Calling the woman was out, too, because she—Rebecca—had no idea what the woman's real name was, or where she lived. "The less you know, the better off we'll both be," the woman had said.

What a sticky situation this was turning into.

EIGHT

The man on the phone was clearly agitated. "Mr. Biergarten, I have a problem. *We* have a problem." The man spoke breathlessly, as if near panic. "I desperately need your help."

Ryerson asked the man's name.

"Jack Lutz," the man answered. "My wife's name is Stevie. We've read about you, we know about you—who in Boston doesn't? And I've talked to the police, of course. They're doing what they can, but it's not enough. They don't know where to begin, for God's sake—"

"I'm sorry, Mr. Lutz," Ryerson cut in, "but you'll have to tell me what this is about."

Silence.

"Mr. Lutz?" Ryerson coaxed.

"I thought you'd simply . . . *know*," Jack Lutz said, clearly astonished.

"It doesn't work that way," Ryerson said.

"But you're supposed to be psychic. Maybe I have the wrong person. Is there another Ryerson Biergarten in Boston?"

"No." Ryerson sighed. "I'm the only one."

Silence.

"If you could tell me why you're calling, Mr. Lutz, I can tell you if I can help."

A moment's silence. "It simply seems odd that I should have to tell you anything . . ." A pause. "Stevie's missing."

"Yes?" Ryerson coaxed.

"That's my wife. Stevie."

"And she's missing. Yes. Please go on."

"I wasn't going to call you, Mr. Biergarten. I really don't believe in any of this supernatural mumbo jumbo. But I'm desperate, and desperate people—"

"Where are you calling from?" Ryerson cut in; he wanted to get Lutz back to the point.

"Where am I calling from?" Lutz seemed surprised. "I'm calling from home. Is that important?"

"Did your wife disappear there? Was she at home when you last saw her?

"Not exactly." He paused. "Listen, why are you asking these questions? Have you decided to help us?"

"I've decided nothing, Mr. Lutz." Ryerson received phone calls about missing people at least once a week. "You say you've contacted the police?"

"That's right. They don't know where to begin. I *told* you that. I mean, there's someone out there at this very moment, but he's simply going over the same ground again and again—"

"The place where your wife disappeared, you mean?"

"Of course." Lutz paused. "Mr. Biergarten, I have to tell you that you're not filling me with optimism. You seem to be picking up nothing at all from me. I was hoping that you had at least read about Stevie's disappearance in the newspaper."

"No, Mr. Lutz."

"Don't you *read* the newspaper, Mr. Biergarten?"

The man was trying Ryerson's patience; Ryerson could hear the desperation in the man's voice, but he—Ryerson—had found that working with someone he disliked was a barrier to his psychic abilities. Ryerson said, "I'm sorry, Mr. Lutz, but you may have expected too much from me. Perhaps it's in your best interests, and in the best interests of your wife, to trust the police in this matter."

"That's probably good advice," Lutz said, and hung up.

Sam Goodlow thought, *Yes. It's true. It must be. I'm dead. Gone. Deceased. Departed. Stiff. Kaput.*

But if that were really true, it wasn't so bad. He was comfortable. He was in familiar surroundings. He felt as if he had found exactly the right position for sleep, had eaten well and was sated, had no needs. What better way was there to *be?* No heaven, no hell. Only comfort and satiation for all that was left of time.

He wondered why he still had a body. Weren't bodies designed simply for the use of the spirit? And wasn't he simply spirit, now? So what was he doing with a body attached?

He wondered if it were someone else's body and he was possessing it. The idea frightened him. Someone else's consciousness, soul, and psyche could be lurking behind his. It was creepy. He shuddered.

Who was he, he wondered, and why was he dead?

Was he dead?

Was he alive? If there were any real way of knowing, shouldn't *he* know? Was his name really Sam Goodlow, and, if so, what did it mean?

Was his hair really as red as it looked reflected in the window, or was that some trick of the light?

Could he be Irish?

What talents did he have that he might make use of now?
Now?
And if he had talents, had he always used them?
Did he dream?
Was he sleeping? Was he alive and sleeping? Dead and sleeping?
Why did he feel wet?
Were his eyes as green as they looked reflected in the window? Did he need to blink? If so, why? Was there a biological reason for it? Did he have a biology? Were there guts inside him? Could he bleed? Sneeze? Fall down and break something?
Was there anything to break?
Could he experience pain?
Pain?
Suddenly, he felt exhausted.

"I'm sorry I hung up like that," Jack Lutz said over the phone. "I . . . lose myself sometimes. I'm sure you understand, Mr. Biergarten."

Ryerson thought he heard the hint of an apology in Lutz's tone, but it was clear that the man was not accustomed to apologizing.

Ryerson said, "Is someone from the police department with you now, Mr. Lutz?"

"You mean right now? No. They've gone."

"Could you tell me the name of the officer assigned to you, then?"

There was a moment's pause, then Lutz said, "It's a woman. She's a lieutenant, I think. Tall woman, dresses well, attractive, but I'm afraid I don't remember—"

"Her name's Lenore Wilson," Ryerson cut in.

"Yes," Lutz said. "That's right."

"She's very capable, Mr. Lutz. I've worked with her on a number of occasions—"

"She thinks that Stevie's been murdered, Mr. Biergarten. I think she even believes that *I* had something to do with it."

Ryerson gave a moment to silence. Then he asked, "Did you?"

"No." Lutz's answer was quick, without hesitation. "Stevie and I were on a walk, she went into a little . . . hunter's cabin, I guess you'd call it, and then she was gone. I told *them* that—the police—and they didn't believe me."

"Are you being charged?"

"I don't know. I don't think so. Wouldn't they tell me if they were going to charge me, Mr. Biergarten?"

"How long has your wife been missing?"

A short pause. "Two days. She disappeared Wednesday morning. I called the police almost immediately."

"You looked for her?"

"Of course I looked for her. I tore that damned place apart, Mr. Biergarten. I looked outside. I looked everywhere. Then I called the police and they came over right away."

"They didn't tell you that you had to wait forty-eight hours before filing a missing persons report?"

"Mr. Biergarten"—he sounded exasperated—"it wasn't as if she went out to the store and didn't come back. I was *with* her, for God's sake. She went into that hunter's cabin and she didn't come out. The cops thought that was pretty unusual. In retrospect, I suppose they thought I was lying—"

"Could you give me your address, Mr. Lutz."

Another short pause. "You're going to help me?"

"I'd like to have a look at this hunter's cabin myself, if that's all right."

Lutz said, "Of course it is," and gave Ryerson his address.

This, thought Stevie Lutz, was a very good place to be, this place of her childhood, and she did not stop to wonder how she had gotten here.

Being here was gift enough.

Here was her mother and father, her little dog, her house in the country—a sad gray mist surrounded it—the pond she swam in, the clear blue sky, and the smells—hay newly mown, pine tar, and, underlying, the tangy smell of the earth itself, the odor of clay.

And there she was—twelve years old, cocky and swaggering in jeans and flannel shirt, looking tough and rural and able to take care of herself as well as anyone.

She frowned. Jack had come into her life during her twelfth year.

A woman appeared from the gray mist that surrounded the house. The woman walked quickly, purposefully, and as she approached, Stevie could see that her eyes were large, brown, and beguiling, and Stevie remembered the other woman who had also appeared from the mist, and had left her light-headed—that woman had been tall, black haired, large breasted.

This woman carried a book in her hand.

"Who are you?" Stevie said.

The woman did not answer. Her beguiling smile tightened. She still walked quickly, with purpose.

"Stay away from me!" Stevie shouted.

"It's so good you've come here to us," the woman said. She was within arm's reach, and the sad gray mist that surrounded the house had advanced with her so that now the house, the pond, the little dog, the twelve-year-old in jeans and flannel shirt, were gone.

"Stay away!" Stevie shouted.

But the woman walked into her. Through her.

NINE

Nobody's going to go up there?" said the woman whom some knew as Violet McCartle to the big man standing in the archway between the living room and foyer. "Of course someone's going to go up there. When they inspect a house, they inspect everything."

The big man frowned. "So what you're saying is, *I* have to go up there, right?"

"Precisely."

He sighed. "I'd rather not do that. I mean, you know what's up there."

"Yes, I do. And I understand your reticence. But *you* put it there, against my wishes, so *you* have to bring it down and put it somewhere else."

"Like where?"

"That's not my decision, is it? I must say, however, that it was abominably stupid of you to bring it here in the first place."

"I figured this was the best place," protested the big man. "You wanted it to look like a disappearance."

"We've had this discussion before. I'm simply telling you that I want that thing moved before the week is out, is that clear?"

The big man looked miserable. "Sure. It's clear."

* * *

It took Jack Lutz and Ryerson twenty minutes to hike to the area of the hunter's cabin, where Stevie had last been seen. Lutz pointed at the roof, visible above the weeds. "There it is, Mr. Biergarten. It's not locked; at least I don't believe it is. It's possible that the police put some kind of lock on it, I don't know. If they did, then there's no way in." He paused. "I can't go over there. I'm sure you understand."

"I do," Ryerson said.

Lutz looked surprised. "Do you?" He squinted up at Ryerson because the sun was in his eyes. "I've got to get back to the house," he continued. He seemed very agitated. "I'm sorry, Mr. Biergarten. I can't stay here with you. You'll be able to find your way back, won't you?"

Ryerson said, "I'll be all right, Mr. Lutz. I'll be able to find my way."

"Of course you will," Lutz said vaguely. He glanced at the cabin's roof again, then, without another word, started back to his house.

Ryerson found that there was no lock, only a yellow ribbon marked CRIME SCENE—DO NOT ENTER across the cabin's only door. He pushed the door open and stepped under the ribbon, into the cabin. The door swung shut behind him. He reached, pulled it open again, looked for a light switch. There was none. He pulled the door open all the way, so it stood against the front wall.

He noticed the smell, here. The smell of the ocean. Salt air. Fish. And, beneath it, a tangy, earthy smell that he couldn't place. The mixture of smells wasn't cloying or off-putting. It was unusual, out-of-place, and he thought it might not be a part of the atmosphere of the little structure at all. Perhaps it was wafting in from outside, although the ocean was several dozen miles east.

There were no windows here and Ryerson found this not only odd but discomforting. Perhaps this wasn't a hunter's cabin after all. Perhaps it was merely a storage shed.

Except for a chair, it was unfurnished and empty. The floor was made of dirt. He looked at it. The dirt—in what sunlight filtered in from outside—was very dark. He bent over, touched it, rolled it between his thumb and forefinger. The dirt was smooth and soft, like pudding. There was no graininess to it. *Odd,* he thought.

A long rectangular patch of bright sunlight illuminated it and, ironically, made it difficult to see, because of the near total darkness in the rest of the place.

He got down on one knee and saw that there were no footprints in the dirt, not even his own.

He swept his hand lightly over it. Marks appeared in it from his fingers, but then, in moments, were gone, as if he were sweeping his hand over the surface of a pond.

He straightened. He felt dizzy; his footing was suddenly uncertain, as if he were on an invisible tightrope.

He needed to leave this place. He felt unsafe in it.

He lurched forward, toward the door, toward the daylight, but got nowhere. As he approached the open doorway—as he put one foot in front of the other—he got no closer to it. The doorway was nearly close enough to touch; he thought that he could *leap* through it. But he was stuck. His feet moved, he had forward motion, but he thought that he might as well be trying to move closer to a mirage.

He stopped moving. He was still dizzy, and he knew its source, now. Uncertainty. This place was an illusion—the walls, the doorway, the dirt. It existed only because he thought that it existed, because it *insinuated* itself on him.

It was a mirage, an illusion, and he was stuck in it. And whatever the reality was here, he was stuck in it, too.

Or it was holding him.

Sam Goodlow woke on his little green cot in his office on the south side of Boston and knew that he was dead.

There were no two ways about it. He was dead, and he was still on the earth, and regardless of the fact that things were not supposed to *be* this way, it was the way that things had turned out, and he knew—without knowing why he knew—that there was nothing he could do about it.

He was on the earth. He was stuck here, something was keeping him here. He could feel it. It was like a physical weight, a strong hand on the top of his head holding him down.

He sat up on his green cot and swung his feet around to the floor. They hit with a satisfying *whump*. He smiled.

He opened his hands and brought them sharply together. They made a clapping noise.

He smiled again. "Good," he whispered.

He had things to do. And sooner or later he thought he would find out what those things were.

"Mr. Biergarten?" Ryerson heard from outside the cabin.

Ryerson called back, "Stay away. Don't come in here, Mr. Lutz."

"What's wrong?" Lutz called.

Ryerson stared hard into the tall sunlit grasses beyond the doorway. He hoped to see Jack Lutz. The man would be an anchor for him, a real part of the real world that he—Ryerson—usually inhabited and so badly needed now. But the sound of Lutz's voice indicated that he was not close by.

"Mr. Biergarten?" Lutz called.

Ryerson leaped toward the doorway. He went through it, through the yellow police ribbon.

"Jesus Christ!" Lutz shouted.

Ryerson found himself in sunlight, in the tall grasses outside the cabin. He heard Lutz coming toward him. "Mr. Biergarten, are you all right?"

Ryerson was on his stomach. He glanced behind at the cabin doorway, then at Lutz, who was above him now. "Don't go in there, Mr. Lutz."

"You're bleeding," Lutz said.

"I am?"

"Yes. Your forehead."

Ryerson touched his forehead, looked at his fingers, saw blood, remembered hitting the doorjamb. "It's okay," he said.

Lutz produced a handkerchief from his pocket and offered it to Ryerson, who took it and dabbed at the blood with it.

"You'll need stitches," Lutz said.

Ryerson looked at the cabin doorway again. He said nothing.

TEN

Midmorning, the following day, Ryerson answered the door-bell but found no one at his door.

He stepped out onto the little wedge-shaped open porch and looked right and left down the street. There was an old couple walking not far away; their backs were to him and the man's gray head was bobbing animatedly beneath his red umbrella as he talked to the woman. No one else was on the rain-soaked street.

Creosote appeared beside Ryerson on the porch and whimpered his confusion. The dog often read the man as well as the man read the dog. Ryerson glanced at him. "Someone's come into the house, pup."

Creosote snorted, sneezed. Ryerson got down on his haunches and scratched the dog's ears; Creosote tilted his head into Ryerson's hand to ask for more.

Ryerson was uneasy. He believed in ghosts because he'd spoken with them. He knew something of the world they existed in because he had been a part of it, if briefly. And he was uneasy now because what little he knew about the world of the dead told him only how very ignorant he was.

Rebecca Meechum said to Jenny Goodlow, over the telephone, "So he knows nothing? He's not going to help you?"

Jenny Goodlow answered, "As I said, I didn't *ask* him to help. I think he's a fraud. And I don't think it's any of your business anyway."

"You're being very uncivil, Jenny," Rebecca said. "My God, we were almost . . . sisters." Rebecca chuckled shortly.

Jenny hung up.

The beguiling dark-eyed brunette sat alone on the train. She was reading a paperback book, and Guy Squires thought it would be all right to sit with her because most of the other seats were taken.

He sat beside her, glanced at her luxurious shoulder-length hair, and said "Hello" in the stiff but polite way that he imagined strangers seated next to one another on trains were supposed to say hello. She looked up from her book, smiled vaguely at him, then looked away.

"Good book?" Guy Squires asked.

She glanced at him again. "Sorry?"

He nodded at the book. "Good book?"

She shook her head. "Not very. It's about a vampire who ages, and that's something vampires simply don't do, isn't it." She shrugged. "So I don't believe a word of it."

"Then why read it?"

"Because it amuses me to read." She paused. "Do you read?"

"Only timetables," Guy Squires answered. "And the stock market report, of course." He was letting her know, in his subtle way, that he was a man accustomed to dealing with money.

The brunette looked appraisingly at him a moment, then sighed. "Too bad. I like men who really read."

"I used to read," Guy Squires told her hurriedly. "Hell, I read all the time. I read whatever I could get hold of.

You couldn't *tear* me away from anything with words on it." He grinned nervously because he was lying and was sure that she could tell. "I once read *War and Peace* and *The Rise and Fall of the Roman Empire* in one sitting, if you can believe it." He paused a half second, then hurried on, "And . . . and I even *wrote* a book once. It wasn't a long book. It was pretty short. Six hundred pages, I guess. Not so long that you would have to set aside a great deal of time to read it . . ."

The brunette cut in, "Then you're a writer. How exciting." She seemed suddenly animated. "What was it about?—this book of yours."

"What was it about?" He grinned nervously again. "Well, it was about a group of people, I guess. And they were . . . they had a kind of conflict—"

"Conflict? I love conflict. It's what life is all about, wouldn't you agree?"

"Of course," Guy Squires said. "Conflict. Where would we be without conflict?" He thought that he was on a roll, now, that he had gotten onto her wavelength. Lord only knew what would follow. He hurried on, "Conflict makes us all . . . human, doesn't it? I . . . I *read* about it all the time—"

"You said you didn't read," she cut in, pouting.

He stared dumbly at her a moment. She seemed very disappointed, suddenly, even annoyed. "Yes, yes," he stammered. "Not since last week. Only timetables and stock market reports since then. No time to read purely for . . ." He cast about in his brain for the word she had used. "Amusement. No time. Too much work, dammit. Too much making money." He grinned nervously. "I hate it, really. This need to make money. You can make only so much and then it becomes . . . redundant." He smiled; that surely had been a remark to remember. He chattered on, as if accustomed to making memorable remarks, "So, I haven't actually read anything for amusement since last week. It amuses me to read. Mysteries, science fiction, romances, the whole . . . gamut, everything. I once read *Collier's Encyclopedia—*"

"Would you like to come home with me?" the brunette cut in.

Guy Squires' mouth dropped open. "You mean it?" he asked breathlessly.

"Obviously, you're a real reader," said the brunette.

"I am, I am."

Ryerson stood in his office doorway, finger poised on the light switch, and looked at the man seated in his desk chair. The man's back was turned.

"Can we leave the light off?" the man asked.

"Of course," Ryerson answered. He could see only the back of the man's head, a wild mop of dark hair—it might have been red, he thought.

"Do you know me?" the man said.

"I don't know the back of your head. Especially in the dark."

"Do you know my voice?"

"I've never heard it, no," Ryerson answered. The man's voice was deep, but not baritone. It had a strained quality which suggested, strangely, that the man wasn't accustomed to speaking.

"Do any names come to you?" the man asked.

"Listen," Ryerson answered, "I could ask you these same questions—"

"You're Ryerson Biergarten," the man cut in. "I know that much, anyway." He seemed to be pleading.

Ryerson turned on the light.

There was no reaction from the man. Ryerson could see that his guess about the man's hair color had been correct; it was red.

Ryerson turned the light off.

"Thank you," the man said.

"For what?"

"For leaving the light off."

Ryerson took a couple of steps into the room. He stopped. He smelled the ocean. He had also smelled the ocean at Jack Lutz's cabin, he remembered. He asked, "Why are you here?"

The man answered at once, "I thought you'd know."

Ryerson was uncertain how to interpret this, whether the man was, indeed, asking why he was here, or whether the man knew why he was here and was being coy.

"I don't understand what you're saying," Ryerson told him.

"I'm not sure," the man said.

"What aren't you sure of?"

"Do you know?"

Ryerson sighed. "If you're playing a game—"

"I don't believe so," the man said. "I don't know. What do I know?"

Ryerson got the uneasy feeling that the man's question was genuine and that he—the man—actually felt that Ryerson could answer it.

"Where have you come from?" Ryerson asked.

"Did you turn on the light a moment ago?" the man asked.

"Yes."

"I only remember it now. Is that odd?"

"I don't understand," Ryerson said.

"I believe that my name is Sam Goodlow," the man said. "Do you know that name?"

Ryerson didn't answer. He was suddenly afraid.

Creosote came into the room and stood next to Ryerson, gaze upturned.

"Sam Goodlow," the man said. "I would face you, I would swivel around in your chair here, but I can't, and I wish I could."

Creosote wheezed.

Ryerson's mouth went dry.

"Mr. Biergarten?" the man said.

"Yes?" Ryerson managed.

"But what is the question?" the man said. "Who knows?"

Creosote turned his flat face toward the voice of the man and cocked his head.

Ryerson came forward quickly and leaned over the front of his desk.

The man in the chair turned around at once and faced him.

Ryerson screamed and ran from the room.

Creosote followed.

Sam Goodlow stared at the empty doorway and wondered what in the hell he had done.

ELEVEN

G uy Squires and the beguiling dark-eyed brunette got off the train together and took a taxi to 114 Troy Street, on Boston's lower east side.

"You *live* here?" Guy Squires asked, flabbergasted.

The brunette, who was clutching her bad paperback book in her right hand and had her left arm around Guy Squires' waist, answered, "I do. Yes. Up there, on the top floor."

The building they were looking at was a narrow, gray, late-Victorian town house which had—many years earlier, Guy Squires imagined—seen better days. It was sandwiched between two squat brown brick buildings. Both buildings bore NO TRESPASSING and FOR SALE signs.

The brunette's building also bore a FOR SALE sign. The sign was yellowed from age and weathering and the real-estate broker's name was barely readable.

Troy Street was short and narrow, and Guy Squires noticed that he and the brunette were the only people on it.

"Well, let's go up," chirped the brunette, took her arm from around Guy Squires' waist, and grabbed hold of his hand.

Guy Squires resisted. He felt uneasy. The street and the

building, the decay and the abandonment made him uneasy. And the brunette made him uneasy, too, though he wasn't sure why. Perhaps because she simply didn't *look* like she belonged here. She looked like she belonged on the upper west side.

"I'm not sure about this," he said.

The brunette laughed. It was an easy laugh, quick and believable, and Guy Squires smiled in response. "This is where I come when I want to be alone," the brunette told him. "I have a place on the upper west side, too, of course. But it's so stuffy there, wouldn't you agree?"

Guy Squires nodded and began to speak, but the brunette went on, "I know this doesn't look like much. But at least there's no one around. We won't want for privacy." She gave him a coy look.

Guy Squires nodded again, with enthusiasm, and said, "Yeah, privacy." He realized that he needed to use a bathroom.

And they went, hand in hand, up the moldering steps of the Victorian town house, through the front doors, inside, and up three flights of lousy stairs to the third floor.

The brunette pushed open a door marked 3c.

Guy Squires said, as the door opened, "You don't lock it?"

"I don't need to," the brunette cooed. "No one bothers me. No one's ever bothered me. They don't dare." She gave him another coy look. "Go on in. Please." And she held her arm out to indicate the apartment.

Again, Guy Squires became uneasy. He could see only darkness inside the apartment. There weren't even any grayish lumps where chairs or couches would be. "It's too dark," he said.

"Silly me," said the brunette, reached around him, and

flicked on a light switch, bathing the apartment in bright light from an overhead fixture. "Is that better?" she said.

But it wasn't.

The apartment was bare. There were dust-covered floors and tall, grimy windows and hideous velvet wallpaper sporting plump, pink cherubs. But no furniture.

Guy Squires asked, "You live here?" He noticed an odd smell from her. It was subtle and unmistakable—the tangy smell of the earth.

"Not exactly," she answered. "Please. Go in. I'll read to you. I'd love to read to you. I've been reading for a very long time."

He glanced at her. He thought that her looks had changed. Her dark eyes had lost some of their color. And her luxurious shoulder-length hair looked longer, wilder.

"Go on in," she said once more, and she attempted another coy look. But it worked badly. The line of her mouth was too hard and thin, and her eyes were too narrow.

Guy Squires said, "I'm afraid this was a mistake."

"Mistake," echoed the brunette. "Mistake," she said again. "No mistake, Jack." And she put her hand in the small of his back and pushed him into the room.

He stumbled, went facedown on the bare floor, turned his head, looked openmouthed at her as she came in through the doorway.

She was holding the bad paperback book in front of her as she glided toward him. Her hair had grown and was the length of her body; it caressed her—it was *alive.* And as she approached, as she held the bad paperback book in front of her like a weapon, she leaned over and he saw that her eyes were blank, that they bore no color at all, and that her mouth was lipless and impossibly wide—it terminated at the sides of her head, like the mouth of a toad.

And she said, as she bent over him and he stared wide-
eyed at her, as his full bladder let go because of his fear,
"I'm going to read to you. And you're going to listen,
dammit!"

Ryerson Biergarten could not clearly remember what had
sent him screaming from his office on the second floor of his
town house. He remembered a face, but indistinctly, as if it
were covered by a stocking.

He remembered little else. He remembered nothing of the
conversation he had had with the man who owned that face,
though he remembered that there *had* been a conversation.
Oblique and cryptic.

He knew well enough why he couldn't remember what
had happened only moments earlier. He was protecting
himself from something fearful and odd and unexplainable.
If his clocks suddenly began moving counterclockwise, he
would have the same reaction. He would tell himself that his
clocks were moving clockwise, although his inner self would
know better. His inner self, after all, was much better
equipped to handle such things. It was connected to the
real, unpredictable, anarchic universe in a way that his
outer self wasn't. It was that way with everyone, he knew.
He wasn't special.

With the eye of his memory, he sought to peel away the
stocking that covered the face. He thought that it was a
male face, and that surely it had been hideous; otherwise he
wouldn't have run screaming from it.

Creosote stood beside him. He glanced down at the dog
but said nothing. The dog's flat, gummy face could have
been easier to look at, he thought, than the one behind the
stocking.

Creosote whimpered.

Ryerson looked away.

He was in his kitchen. He didn't remember coming here. He didn't even particularly like it here. He knew that people congregated in kitchens because they were places that were often filled with warmth and with friendly smells. But his kitchen was bare and utilitarian, and he didn't eat in it often because there was no one to eat in it with.

He couldn't peel away the stocking that covered the face in his memory. He saw Creosote's face beneath it—round, dark eyes, tiny fangs, and triangular patterns of black and white fur. He grinned.

The face in his memory cleared and grinned back. He gasped. But he did not scream. That, he thought, was a beginning, at least. The next step would be communication.

The prospect made him weak in the knees.

Sam Goodlow thought, *I am in another man's chair, in another man's house, and I've just scared the hell out of him.* He wondered how he had done it. He wondered what there could be about him that would make a grown man scream and run away.

And he wondered why he was here, in that man's chair, in that man's house.

Why was he *anywhere?*

He was dead, for God's sake.

Wasn't he?

Maybe not.

But of course he was. He remembered the mammoth Lincoln Town Car coming at him, the beefy driver grinning at him, remembered the sky coming down, the road coming up.

Then nothing.

Clear enough. He was dead. (Unless he had survived, somehow.)

And he was sitting in another man's chair, in another man's house.

Why? Because the man knew him? Because he knew the man? Because they were friends?

Who knows? he wondered.

And answered himself that the man knew, of course.

He rose from the desk chair, crossed the room, and went out into the hallway. "Hello?" he called. "Who's here? Is someone here?"

This was stupid, he thought. The man who owned this house had to be here, unless he'd run screaming out into the street.

A tall mirror stood at the end of the hallway, not far off, and Sam looked at himself in it.

What he saw there made him shudder.

The phone rang, and Ryerson turned his head quickly toward it. The phone was in the foyer, down a short hallway from the kitchen. He thought briefly about ignoring it, but went down the hallway and answered it anyway because he had never been able to ignore a ringing telephone.

Jack Lutz, clearly upset, said, "It's my wife, Mr. Biergarten. It's Stevie. She's come back."

Ryerson knew from the man's tone that *She's come back* did not mean what it seemed to mean. "Go on," he said.

"Mr. Biergarten, she's here, now. I can *see* her, for God's sake."

"You're at home, Mr. Lutz?"

"She's *looking* at me! But I don't think she can see me. I'm sure she can't see me. I *know* she can't see me!"

"Do you smell anything unusual, Mr. Lutz?"

"For Christ's sake, she's looking right at me and she can't see me—"

"Mr. Lutz, do you *smell* anything unusual?"

"Yes. Salt air. Fish." A pause. "Wet clay."

"Yes, *Ms.* Erb," said the woman who called herself Violet McCartle. "I'm fully aware of what dumping my stock portfolio might do to the market, but it is, after all, *my* portfolio, and I can do with it what I wish. And I wish to unload it."

Janice Erb sighed and poured herself another cup of coffee.

"You may pour me a cup, too," said the woman who called herself Violet McCartle.

Janice looked confusedly at her. "When did you start drinking coffee again?"

A moment's silence. Janice noticed that the woman looked suddenly bewildered. She said, "Didn't you say your doctors recommended against it?"

The woman nodded. "Yes, but, as you can see, Ms. Erb, I'm doing much better. Once again, I'm ambulatory. My blood pressure has returned to normal, and so I have resumed some old and very pleasurable habits." She withdrew a pack of cigarettes from her cavernous black leather purse. "Do you mind?" She lit up at once and glanced about for an ashtray. There was none. She flicked her ash on the floor, nodded at the coffeepot and said, "Light, no sugar."

TWELVE

S am Goodlow shuddered at his reflection because he saw it with such numbing clarity that it scared him.

He could not remember seeing his reflection so clearly before, and he stared at it now for a long time without moving and thought, *So this is what other people see when they see me.*

He remembered looking at his reflection before, but it had never been the same as it was now. Prior to this moment, looking at his reflection had been like trying to hear his own voice when he spoke. He had always heard it through the passageways, bone, and muscle of his own head, and it was not what other people heard. Looking at his reflection had been the same sort of thing. He had always seen what he wanted to see, what he had *hoped* to see. He had been kind to himself, for his own sake.

But there he was, now. Big and oafish and vulnerable looking. No macho man. Barely more than an infant in a double-X suit. It was what other people saw, and he had never known it.

He looked away.

He turned around.

There was a stairway close by and he could hear someone talking from below.

He listened for a while, uncertain that he recognized the voice, and started down the stairway.

"But now she's gone," Jack Lutz said. "I can't see her anymore. She vanished, like that, my God, like that, pff, Mr. Biergarten . . ."

"It may not have been her you were seeing," Ryerson said.

"But it was. I saw her. It was Stevie."

Ryerson hesitated. He wasn't sure what he was suggesting. Ideas often came to him that way—not fully formed. Often, they stayed that way. Often, they went nowhere. He said, "I'm coming over there, Mr. Lutz. I'll arrive within the hour. Promise me you won't go near the place where your wife disappeared."

"Of course," Lutz said. "I won't go anywhere near it. I haven't been *able* to go anywhere near it."

"Yes, good," Ryerson said, and hung up.

Moments later, with Creosote in his arms, he was leaving the house.

Sam Goodlow stood in front of the door, watched Ryerson go, and became very confused. Man and dog had passed through him as if he were no more substantial than air. Good Lord, he and the man had been *talking* together only minutes earlier, and now the man could walk through him and apparently think nothing of it.

What was the protocol here? Who was supposed to acknowledge whom? Would there be times when he—Sam—would be unable to see him—Ryerson? Or did it work only one way? Were the living usually unable to see the dead? Did the dead have perfect vision and ultimate wisdom? But clearly they didn't. At least *he* didn't or he wouldn't be asking these questions of himself.

Maybe there were people in the house even now and he couldn't see or hear them. Maybe *they* were looking at him and wondering what sort of creature he was.

The idea made his skin crawl.

And then he was in the third seat of Ryerson's 1948 "Woody" station wagon.

It was the twin of a car that Ryerson had owned two years earlier. He had totalled that car and replaced it with this one, because his parents had owned a Woody, and going places in it had been among the happiest and most secure times of his life.

This new Woody was gray, it sported real wood siding, its motor hummed as well as any forty-five-year-old motor could hum, and Ryerson drove the car badly because it was all but impossible for him to ignore the barrage of psychic input that came his way from other drivers.

Creosote sat beside him, buckled into a toddler's seat. It had taken a while for Ryerson to teach the dog to stay put, but he sat well in it, now, and Ryerson thought the dog might even be aware that it was for his own good.

Ryerson was not aware of his other passenger.

Sam Goodlow was aware only that he was in a car on a narrow country road, and that the car was moving much too slowly.

This is what the cop saw: an ancient Ford station wagon in mint condition; a driver and passenger (who was sitting very stiffly in the wagon's third seat); a long line of cars, bearing angry drivers, behind the wagon.

The cop waited for the last car to pass, pulled out, and rode the narrow, sloping shoulder until he was to the right of the Woody. He honked his horn. Ryerson appeared to pay no attention. He turned on his siren. Still, Ryerson appeared to pay no attention.

The cop swore under his breath and pulled in front of the Woody, but—not wanting to be rear-ended—did not stop.

Cop, Ryerson thought.

Stupid son of a bitch! thought the cop.

Angry cop, Ryerson thought.

"He's pulling us over," said Sam Goodlow from the third seat.

Ryerson snapped his gaze to the rearview mirror. He saw the same bizarre face there that he had seen looking up at him from his desk chair and he screamed again, swerved the car into the left lane, lurched back, and jammed his foot into the brake pedal. The Woody—its brakes kept in good repair—stopped almost at once.

The angry driver just behind Ryerson, who had been following at half a car-length, slammed into the rear end of the Woody. The other cars, following at more prudent distances, stopped in time.

The cop kept going for several seconds, unaware of what was happening behind him.

"Dammit!" Ryerson whispered.

"Sorry," said Sam Goodlow.

The cop looked in his rearview mirror, saw what had happened, cursed again, stopped, backed up.

"Dammit, I can see *through* your head," Ryerson said to Sam Goodlow.

"I don't understand," Sam said.

"Your brains, dammit, and your—What are those?—

your sinus cavities, your damned sinus cavities. And your optic nerves—"

"You're kidding."

Ryerson heard a loud knock at his window. He ignored it. He said to Sam Goodlow, "It's why I screamed. I'm not *used* to seeing people the way I'm seeing you."

"Roll down the window," said the cop.

"What do they look like?" Sam asked. "My brains, I mean. Are they like fat worms?"

The cop tapped harder on the window.

"Can't you see them for yourself?" Ryerson asked. "Look in the mirror."

Sam shook his head. "It's not the same. When I look in the mirror I . . . it makes me cringe. I don't *see* any brains, like you do."

"Open the goddamned window," the cop demanded, "or I'll break it open!"

Creosote, sitting primly in the toddler's car seat, wheezed and whimpered.

Ryerson sighed, turned to the face of the cop, which was all but smashed into the glass, and rolled the window down.

The cop snarled, "What in the name of all that's holy are you *doing*, mister? You drive like you're a hundred years old!" He looked toward the back of the Woody. His snarl drooped. "And where the hell is your passenger?"

Ryerson looked into the backseat. Sam Goodlow's eyes and mouth and brains and sinus cavities looked back.

Ryerson cringed and looked at the cop. "No passenger," he said.

Creosote gurgled—his wheezy approximation of a growl.

"The hell you say," the cop snarled, and walked to where he could see more clearly into the third seat. He leaned over, put his face against the glass, saw nothing. He came back to

Ryerson's window and asked for Ryerson's license and registration, which Ryerson produced quickly, having been asked for those items more than once in his driving career.

At that moment, two twelve-year-old boys were walking in a densely wooded area twenty miles west of Boston when they came upon a strange mound of earth that looked as if it had been recently put there.

"I'll betcha someone's *buried* in it!" offered one of the boys.

"Naw," said the other boy. "It's just a termite mound. I seen them on TV, and they look like that."

"You think so?" said the first boy, clearly disappointed.

The second boy shrugged. "We could dig it up and find out."

The first boy wasn't sure about this idea. If the mound was indeed a burial mound, then when they dug in it, they'd find someone's body, and he didn't know how he'd react to that. He might drop over dead, or he might faint, and that would be really embarrassing. If the mound was a termite mound, then when they dug in it, they'd get termites all over them, and who knew what termites would do to his skin, considering what they did to wood. He said, "I don't know," in the bored way that boys say it to get other boys onto different pursuits.

But the second boy was intrigued. "I'll bet you think the termites are gonna bitecha!" He shook his head solemnly. "They don't bite."

Both boys had walking sticks in hand. The second boy stepped forward and poked at the mound. The walking stick sank easily into the soft dirt, and the boy withdrew it. He studied the end of the stick and scowled, confused.

The first boy looked at the end of the stick, too.

The second boy shrugged. "Wet," he said.

"Well, it rained last night," the first boy said.

"Yeah," said the second boy. He studied the wet dirt on the end of the stick a moment longer, and then, on impulse, ran to the top of the three-foot-high mound and jumped up and down on it.

In the third seat of Ryerson's Woody Wagon, Sam Goodlow shivered. "Christ, what was that?" he whispered.

Ryerson, while waiting for the cop to issue him a ticket charging him with improper speed and unsafe lane changes, was getting a lecture—about the dangers of driving too slowly—from the driver who had been following at half a car length and had rear-ended him.

Ryerson glanced into the rearview mirror and said, "Problem?"

The driver at his open window said, "Problem? *Problem?* Dammit, but you've got big brass balls, mister!"

Sam nodded grimly at Ryerson and said, "Someone just danced on my grave."

THIRTEEN

So this is how I'm going to die! Guy Squires thought, awestruck. *Starved to death by a demon-woman who reads bad novels aloud endlessly.*

The brunette was smiling coyly at him as she read, as if she were bringing him some secret pleasure. Her eyes, which were once again dark and beguiling, did not move from him to the page she was reading, and Guy Squires supposed that she had read this particular bad novel so many times she'd memorized it.

" 'His death screams were like gunshots in a closed cylinder,' " she read. " 'And the vampire's fangs, as big as walruses, bit into him and made his flesh into cheese.' "

Guy Squires thought many things about her as she read. He thought that she had acquired strength that did not show in her slim body. Perhaps she knew martial arts, which was how she had kept him from overpowering her and leaving this awful place, with its grimy windows and bare floors and velvet wallpaper, and its stale nearly unbreathable air.

And he thought that she was something of a hypnotist, as well, or, at least, that she had the awful power to make him see what was not there, because it was clear that she could not have become the demon that she had seemed to become. Such things simply were not possible.

She sat cross-legged on the bare floor between him and the door as she read. " 'And as his skin became food for the dead, and the flesh of his bones, too, and then the bones, which were sticking out all over his dying body like twigs on an old tree, a tree that was dying, if not dead—' "

Guy Squires had thought of lunging for one of the tall windows just behind him. It was a three story drop, but he could survive it if he fell correctly. If he didn't hit head-first or fall backwards. Hit with his feet and roll. It was the way that paratroopers learned to fall. Hit and roll.

And probably break his goddamned skull, he decided.

Which would, at the last, be preferable to what was probably going to happen to him if he stayed here.

" 'And there were other vampires, too,' " the brunette read. " 'And they were big as blimps, big as dirigibles, which floated at the horizon like lacy clouds making time for rain, which tickled the far horizon like tiny fingers.' "

Jack Lutz said testily, "You told me you'd only be an hour, Mr. Biergarten. It's been almost two hours."

He and Ryerson were just outside Lutz's front door, and were about to walk to the cabin where Stevie Lutz had disappeared.

Ryerson, who was holding Creosote in his arms, began, "I'm sorry," and went on to tell Lutz about the accident, and the ticket; at last, he pointed at the rear end of the Woody and concluded proudly, "There wasn't much damage to my car. She's quite a sturdy old thing. But the other car had to be towed away."

"Certainly," Lutz said, unimpressed, then, looking more

closely at the Woody, which was a good one hundred feet away, said, "Is there someone in your car?"

"Do you see someone?" Ryerson asked, trying to sound neutral.

Lutz squinted at the car. He fished his glasses from his shirt pocket and put them on. At last, he shook his head. "I guess not."

Creosote gurgled, wheezed, snorted.

Lutz gave him a distasteful look. "Your little dog is sick or something, Mr. Biergarten. I'd see a veterinarian if I were you."

"Asthma," Ryerson explained. "It's a fault of the breed."

"Of course," Lutz said, again unimpressed.

Then he and Ryerson and Creosote started down the path which lead to the cabin.

Sam Goodlow lumbered behind them at a safe distance.

"What are you telling me, Mr. Biergarten?" Lutz said five minutes later. They had been walking quickly and were already halfway to the cabin. "Are you telling me you think that hunter's cabin is haunted?"

Ryerson grimaced. "I'm sorry." He scratched Creosote behind the ears because he sensed that the dog had an itch there. Creosote responded by giving him an almost obscenely loving look. "Haunted," Ryerson continued, "is a word I don't much like to use. Saying a place is haunted is like saying someone's *crazy,* don't you think? What does that mean—*crazy?* It could mean any of a number of things. It's more epithet than description. It's the same with 'haunted'—it implies all kinds of nonsense, and I don't think I need to go into what sort of nonsense I'm talking about.

"What is important here, Mr. Lutz, is that your wife has

apparently happened upon what might liberally be called a 'gateway.' It happens more often than anyone realizes, I think. These gateways apparently open at random and close at random; this is only a theory, of course. And I believe that they account for a good percentage of the hundreds of thousands of people who turn up missing every year.

"And I think that what is even more important as regards these gateways is that what 'haunts' us most, is, ultimately, ourselves, our pasts. The world of the hereafter, Mr. Lutz, is doubtless as complex and as—"

"Mr. Biergarten," Lutz cut in, "you sound like you're making a speech. I don't need speeches. I need to find my damned wife."

"Yes," Ryerson said, nonplussed. "I'll do my best."

Asshole! he heard from behind him. He glanced back and saw all the outsides and insides of Sam Goodlow, and Sam Goodlow's mouth grinning at him like the Cheshire cat.

Lutz refused, again, to go into the hunter's cabin. "I'll wait here, Mr. Biergarten, you just . . ."—he fluttered his hand in the air to indicate the cabin—". . . go in there and do whatever it is you do."

Ryerson glanced about. Sam Goodlow was nowhere to be seen.

"Are you listening to me?" Lutz asked.

Ryerson looked down at Lutz, who was squinting at him because the sun was in his eyes. "Do you hear what I'm saying?" Lutz asked.

"Yes, very clearly," Ryerson said. "If you could just watch my dog for a few minutes." He handed Creosote over; Lutz accepted the dog as if he were accepting a bag of manure.

Then Ryerson turned, and went into the cabin.

* * *

It was not as he remembered. There was no pervasive ocean smell. The floor was solid wood; the atmosphere was dry. A hole in the roof—he had not noticed the hole on his previous visit—let in a shaft of bright sunlight.

It was not the place he had visited only a couple of days earlier.

It had changed.

It was earthbound.

From a corner of the little building, Sam Goodlow said, "This is where the asshole's wife disappeared?"

Ryerson lurched upon hearing the voice.

"Sorry," Sam said, and his tone announced that he meant it.

Ryerson glanced quickly about the cabin, from corner to corner. He saw nothing. He said, "I can't see you."

"I can see you."

"Are you trying to hide, Mr. Goodlow?"

Silence.

"Mr. Goodlow?" Ryerson coaxed.

"It's Sam." A pause. "Sam," he repeated, and Ryerson noted a touch of what sounded like reverence in his tone when he said the name. He went on, "And no, I'm not trying to hide. At least, I don't *believe* I am."

Ryerson thought about this a moment. "Are you telling me that you can't control your appearances and disappearances?"

"Apparently not."

"Apparently not what, Sam?" Ryerson asked. He heard a sigh.

"Apparently," Sam explained, "I can't control my appearances and disappearances. It takes a lot of effort simply to stay in one place, Mr. Biergarten."

"Call me Rye."

From outside, Lutz called, "I think your little dog has to pee. What should I do?"

"Just put him down. He'll stay close by."

Sam said, "Your dog loves you."

"My dog *needs* me," Ryerson corrected.

"Whatever passes best for love, he has in abstinence for you," Sam said.

"Abstinence?"

"Abstinence, penitence, abundance, what's the difference?"

Ryerson saw a form emerging in a corner. It was tall, and it was as thin as a water pipe.

"I don't know how I know that, Rye." He seemed confused. The tall thin form in the corner fattened, took the shape of a man. "I don't know how I know anything. It's very confusing being . . . this way. Sometimes, often, in fact, I really don't know if I'm dead or alive. Now, at this moment, that is not so. How could it be so, and me like this?"

Ryerson said, "That is doubtless the same sort of confusion I think we all feel when we are thrust from the womb and into this world."

Silence.

Ryerson felt embarrassed; he wasn't sure why.

He heard a woman's voice. It came from the same corner that Sam's voice had come from. It said, "Don't philosophize about things you've never experienced, Mr. Biergarten."

The mannish form in the corner had not changed. It was tall, stocky, indistinct, but it was much the same form he had come to associate with Sam Goodlow. Ryerson said, "And who are you?"

"What do you mean?"—the woman's voice. "Who am

I?"—Sam's voice. "I'm Sam Goodlow. Sam. Spam. Sam."

"I heard a woman talking," Ryerson said. He hesitated. "You were talking in a woman's voice."

"I was?" He paused. "I don't think I was." Another pause. "Who can hear his own voice, really, Mr. Biergarten?"

From outside, Lutz called, "Your little dog ran off. I can't see him anywhere."

"Shit!" Ryerson whispered. He quickly left the cabin and called to Creosote several times, waited, called again. At last, the dog came running from around the far side of the cabin, leaped into Ryerson's arms, and smothered him with licks and snuggles, while Lutz—obviously offended— looked on.

"Where have you been, little guy?" Ryerson asked. "You act like you haven't seen me for months?"

But Creosote wasn't talking.

Ryerson said, while Creosote snuggled against the underside of his chin, "I'm sorry, Mr. Lutz, but I don't think there's anything I can do here today. This place simply doesn't . . . speak to me anymore. Whatever *was* here has gone somewhere else."

Lutz pursed his lips. "You sound like a damned *fortune-*teller now."

"No, Mr. Lutz"—Ryerson could feel his anger mounting; Lutz had rubbed him the wrong way since their first conversation—"I never claimed to be a fortune-teller. I will continue to do what I can for you, but this place is dead for me, at the moment, and while I know that you are probably skeptical—"

"Yes, yes," Lutz broke in, "well I think that I'm going to be charged in Stevie's disappearance, anyway. So all of this is rather moot, wouldn't you say?" He gave Ryerson a lopsided grin.

"No," Ryerson began, "I wouldn't say it's moot—"

But Lutz turned from him and started for the path that would lead him back to the house.

"A troubled man," Ryerson whispered to Creosote, and followed Lutz.

The tall, mannish form in a corner of the cabin stayed where it was. For the moment, it could do nothing else. It was stuck.

The woman who called herself Violet McCartle looked expectantly at the big man as he came into the living room. "Well?" she said.

The big man said nothing. He sat in a fragile-looking straight-backed chair near her, leaned forward, and looked troubled.

Violet McCartle pressed, "Did you do what I asked you to do, dammit?"

The big man shrugged. "I've started to."

"You've *started* to? What in the hell does that mean? If you started to do it, why in the hell didn't you finish?"

The big man sighed. His face grew pale. "You haven't been up there lately, have you?"

"I've never been up there, actually, and I don't *plan* to go up there, either. But I fail to see how that's germane. How can you expect *me* to do the kinds of things that *you* do? We are equipped, you and I, to do very different kinds of things, and if I must be brutally frank—"

"Jesus," he interrupted, "it's just *awful* up there. I mean . . ." He looked as if he were going to throw up. "It's not just . . . *it*. If that were the case, then maybe I could do

what you want me to do without any problem. But it isn't,
it's—"

"Either you do what I've told you to do or your employment with me will cease. And you know what that means,
right?"

He sighed. "Yes. I know what that means."

"Then we'll have no more discussion of this matter.
You'll do as I've asked, and that will be that."

The big man said nothing. He was remembering what she
had said only moments earlier: "I've never been up there,
actually, and I don't plan to go up there, either."

FOURTEEN

Ryerson said to Jenny Goodlow, over the telephone, "I have made contact with your brother."

"Are you saying that my brother is alive?"

"No, I'm not."

A pause. Then, "You're saying that he's not alive, but that you've made contact with him." It was a statement, not a question.

"I'm saying that I've had contact with him. We've spoken. I've *seen* him, after a fashion."

"You're being very cryptic, Mr. Biergarten."

"Of necessity. You made it clear how you feel about what I do, Miss Goodlow."

"I made it clear how I feel about what you *say* you do. My threshold of willing suspension of disbelief is quite high."

Ryerson smiled.

"You understood that, I assume?" Jenny Goodlow asked.

"Yes. It's a literary phrase, am I right?"

She sighed. "Mr. Biergarten, we appear to be playing games with each other."

"If we are, then I wasn't aware of it. I called as a courtesy to say that I've had contact with your brother. I'm willing to elaborate, if you'd like."

Silence. He waited for a response from her. After half a minute, he heard the sharp click of the phone being hung up.

Guy Squires realized with grim and fearful fascination that the air in this little apartment was growing very stale and that he would not for long be able to breathe it.

He was sitting against a wall. The dark-eyed and beguiling brunette was still sitting cross-legged on the bare wood floor between him and the door, and she was still reading aloud from the bad novel she had been reading from for the past several hours. She was staring at him as she read; she had yet to look at her book.

Guy Squires thought, again, of trying to talk to her. He had tried talking to her a number of times, but she had simply continued reading to him and staring at him. He had pleaded with her to let him go, had told her that he was the father of twin baby girls—it was a lie—and that his wife was ill and in the hospital—also a lie. His pleas had had no effect.

Perhaps the truth.

"I lied to you," he told her, and felt very good and bold for saying it. Surely it would impress her.

She did not react.

For half a second—barely long enough for him to realize it—she was gone and he was the only one in the apartment.

But then she was back, and he went on, "I don't read. I haven't"—he fought for breath as the air seemed to grow stale—"read anything in years. Not since"—another hard-won breath—"I was in high school. And then only what was necessary."

She continued reading: " 'He lifted the room-sized vampire clear off the floor,' " she read, " 'and blood poured over him like wine at a bachelor's party . . .' "

And Guy Squires continued to plead with her, as the oxygen in the room seemed to dissipate, "I am only a . . . man who likes . . . women—"

" 'And the blood turned to putrescence and then to dust and then to nothing, for it had come from nothing, and always had been nothing—' " She vanished again. Longer. But now someone took her place. Another woman. Blond, thin.

"Huh?" said Guy Squires.

The thin, blond woman vanished, replaced by the beguiling woman with the brown eyes, and Guy Squires yelled, "Listen to me, goddammit!" And when she merely continued reading and staring at him, he pushed himself painfully to his feet, lurched toward her, and threw himself past her, toward the doorway. He had expected her to reach out, as she had before, and effortlessly toss him back to where he had been. But she did nothing. She continued reading.

Then Guy Squires was at the door, and he threw it open, looked back, saw the thin, blond woman again, and the beguiling, brown-eyed woman, too, in the same space that the blond woman inhabited.

"Jesus Christ!" he breathed, and within a minute, he was out of the building and down the street.

The early morning air was cool, dark, and moist, and Ryerson wondered for only a moment why he had awakened so abruptly.

He glanced about the bedroom. The tall, narrow windows bore the first blush of morning. He saw little of the rest of the room, only vague lumps that were its furnishings.

"Sam?" Ryerson whispered.

He heard, "I got stuck, Mr. Biergarten." The voice came from near the door. Ryerson looked. He saw darkness.

The voice—not the voice that Ryerson had come to associate with Sam Goodlow; it was sexless, neutral—continued, "I got stuck there. At that place. Where the asshole took us."

"Lutz?"

"Yes. Lutz."

"Stuck how, Sam?"

"Stuck, stuck. Where could I toe, go?" The voice was losing some of its neutrality; it was becoming Sam Goodlow's lazy tenor. At the same time, Ryerson could see a tall, beige shape emerging from the darkness. It fattened, like a cocoon forming. "That's a hell of a space, that place," Sam continued. "You didn't know, you couldn't see. *I* could see."

"What could you see?"

"More than you, for sure. It's my world, after all, the fall, that place, place. Lots of hunger and joy and play, and this and that, and bric-a-brac."

"Can you tell me about it, Sam?"

"Tell you what? What you didn't see and couldn't know? I don't know what I saw. I've never seen it before. What do I compare it to? A spring play, a summer's day, feet of clay. Sometimes I believe that I'm alive, Mr. Biergarten. I get scared and I believe that I'm alive and that I was never dead."

"I understand that, Sam."

"You say you do."

"But I do. I honestly do."

"You're a damned presumptuous son of a bitch, Ryerson." It was the woman's voice again. "You presume to tell me, and who can tell me?" A pause. "I saw what you didn't see and couldn't know, unless you were me, or were like me." Sam's lazy tenor emerged once more. "I can't get it right, nothing, anything, something, even squeaking, and I want to get it right, Mr. Biergarten."

"Do you mean you can't get the voice right, Sam?"

"Sometimes I believe that I am alive, and there I am, alive, hell, I feel . . . pain, I have red snakes, headaches, and my stomach growls. And I don't remember being dead. How *would* I, if I believe that I'm alive. It would be a kind of cosmic recognition, contradiction, wouldn't it? Do you have a Lincoln Town Car, Mr. Biergarten?"

The abrupt change of conversational direction took Ryerson by surprise. After a moment, he said, "No. I have a Woody. You were riding in it, remember?"

"I remember a Lincoln Town Car. Big, fat mother of a car. I'm glad you don't own one. I don't know anyone who does."

"Sam, I sense your confusion—"

The mannish beige form near the door was gone. Ryerson turned on his bedside lamp. He looked frantically about the room. It was empty.

Creosote, asleep at the foot of the bed, awoke and gurgled at him.

Stevie Lutz was exhausted. It confused her.

Here was the past, *her* past, playing out for her. Entertaining her. Re-creating itself for her as if it were playdough and she was able to work magic with her fingers.

Here, at her bidding and control, was her girlhood home, her little dog, the pond she swam in.

Here *she* was. Twelve years old, swaggering, cocky.

So much of the past.

And so much exhaustion. Down deep. Into the soul. Exhaustion that took her breath away.

As the sad, gray mist swirled around the house and drew steadily closer, slowly but inexorably obliterating her past.

FIFTEEN

Matthew Peters, who had been vacuuming on the first floor of the town house, stuck his head into Ryerson's office and said, "Mr. Biergarten, someone to see you."

"Who is it?" Ryerson asked.

"He wouldn't give me his name. I'll ask again, if you'd like. He says you know him."

Ryerson sighed. "Where is he? Downstairs?"

Matthew nodded. "He's waiting at the front door, actually."

Ryerson considered a moment, then said, "Go ahead and let him in, Matthew. I'll be right down."

"Sure," Matthew said.

Ryerson went to a window that overlooked the front porch. He peered out, saw, beneath the small porch roof, a gray suit sleeve, a hand, a black oxford wing tip.

He went downstairs.

Matthew, waiting in the hallway, gestured toward the living room.

Ryerson went in.

The man in the gray suit was standing near the fireplace. He smiled cordially as Ryerson entered the room. He was tall, athletically built, and he sported a nicely trimmed blond beard and mustache. His vaguely thinning hair was blond and his eyes were a striking pale blue. He was a very good-looking man and seemed, even standing quietly, to be the kind of man who could command much respect.

Ryerson strode forward and offered his hand: "I'm Ryerson Biergarten. Mr. Peters said you wanted to see me?"

The man shook Ryerson's hand firmly. "Yes, Mr. Biergarten. I have a problem, and I believe you can help me solve it. My name's Sam Goodlow."

Ryerson let go of the man's hand. "No you aren't," he said.

The man's cordial smile faded. He looked confused, disappointed. "But I *know* who I am, Mr. Biergarten," he protested.

Ryerson shook his head. "I've met Sam Goodlow. I *know* him."

"But you and I have never met before." The man's smile returned; now, however, he looked bemused, as if Ryerson were playing a game with him. "Look here," the man said, "I can prove who I am." He reached into his suitjacket pocket, produced a wallet, opened it, looked inside. Again he appeared confused. "Good Lord, someone's stolen everything from my wallet. It's empty. There's absolutely nothing in it." He held the wallet open for Ryerson to look. "See. Nothing." He peered into the wallet's several compartments; he was clearly upset. "I don't know how this could have happened. I didn't *leave* it anywhere. I came right here from my office and I *know* that I had money then because I stopped to make a telephone call at a public phone, and I needed change . . ." He rifled through the wallet. "Dammit to hell, this is incredible, a man's personal belongings aren't safe even on his own body—"

Ryerson, seeing the man's obvious and sincere distress, stepped forward and put his hand on the man's shoulder in an attempt to soothe him.

The man lurched away from Ryerson's hand. "Who are you touching? Why do you want to put your hand on me?" He was very angry.

And, all at once, Ryerson realized what was happening. "I'm sorry," he said. He stared at the man for a couple of seconds, then added, "I believe we have much to discuss."

"You aren't going to touch me again, are you?" the man pleaded. His words were in stark contrast to his distinguished good looks; they were words, and tone, that could elicit only pity and confusion.

"Perhaps we could go up to my office," Ryerson suggested. "There are some things you need to be made aware of, Mr. Goodlow."

The woman who called herself Violet McCartle said, "Then you have indeed taken care of the problem? It's not something that I have to be concerned with anymore?"

The big man hesitated before answering. He was a lousy liar, and he knew it. He said, "I did what you told me to do. There is no more problem."

"And if the bank's real-estate inspectors want to come through, then I won't be made to suffer an . . . embarrassment?"

Another hesitation. The big man was amazed that the woman hadn't caught onto his lie. "When are they coming through?" he asked.

"They have made no appointment. When I have a buyer for this mausoleum"—she smiled at her grim joke—"then they'll come through. I must tell you, and I'm sure you're aware of this, that I do not countenance lying. If I were to go up there now and find that you have indeed lied to me, you know how badly it would go for you. Not only would you be out of employment, you would be in very deep trouble with some extremely unpleasant people. I wouldn't want that for you."

He said, "I swear I'm telling the truth."

"Of course you are. You're not a complete idiot."

He bristled. "Someday, I'm going to—" He stopped.

"You're going to what?" she taunted. "Murder me? Bash my head in? Run me over with that ugly car? You like doing that sort of thing, don't you?" She smiled. "I don't think you'll touch me, though. And I'll tell you why. Because I am simply much smarter than you, and in this world, smart people are in control. I *control* you, and you know it."

He said nothing.

Ryerson Biergarten said to the blond man in the gray suit—who stood expectantly in front of the desk while Ryerson, who was seated, cradled Creosote in his arms and idly scratched the dog behind the ears—"I'm sure you believe you are who you say you are. But the sad fact is"—a pause for effect—"you aren't."

The blond man looked uncomprehendingly at Ryerson.

Ryerson went on, "This is very hard to understand," Creosote squirmed so Ryerson could scratch him lower, around his neck, "But you believe you are . . . one of us—"

"Oh, that's very cryptic," said the blond man. "If there's something you want me to know, then simply spit it out."

But Ryerson couldn't spit it out. How could he? This man standing expectantly in front of his desk was convinced that he was alive. ("Sometimes," Sam Goodlow had told him, "I feel like I'm alive. And I *believe* it.") Ryerson put Creosote on the floor, leaned forward over the desk, clasped his hands. "What is it that you wanted to see me about, Mr. Goodlow?"

The man smiled broadly. "Yes, now that's better." He glanced about the office, nodded at a straight chair against the wall to his right. "Can I bring that over?"

"Of course."

The man brought the chair over, sat in it, and crossed his arms at his chest. "I have a job for you, Mr. Biergarten. Someone's following me. I don't know who, or why, but I don't like to be followed. Who would? Every time I turn around, there he is. Big fellow. Awkward looking—oafish looking, really. Red hair, unkempt. My God, the man has the face of an infant, but he's very threatening. I mean by that that he *looks* threatening, Mr. Biergarten. Do you understand?"

Ryerson nodded grimly. "Yes, Mr. Goodlow. I'm afraid that I do."

The man gave Ryerson a quick, quizzical look, then hurried on, "He drives a large car. A fat car. I believe that it's a Lincoln. Every time I turn around, there *it* is, and there *he* is. It's very unnerving. Now I know that you are what's called a *psychic* detective, and I know that this sort of job is not really in your area of expertise, but I feel that you would be a great help to me, nonetheless."

"You may be right."

"Of course I am. I'm a good judge of people, Mr. Biergarten, and I have the clear idea that this is something you could sink your teeth into. Am I right?"

"I already have."

"I'm sure of it. I can see it in your eyes." He stood

abruptly, bent over the desk, offered Ryerson his hand. Ryerson stood, shook his hand.

The man said, "I have other business for now, Mr. Biergarten. But I'll be in touch."

"I'm looking forward to it," Ryerson said.

SIXTEEN

J ack Lutz watched as his wife moved absently about their living room.

It was a big living room. They had bought the house thinking that such a large living room would be a good place to entertain. It was furnished tastefully, in muted shades of brown, gray, and beige, and there was just enough chrome that it did not shock the eye.

Stevie Lutz moved haltingly in this room, through the tasteful furnishings, into the walls, and then out again, and the expression on her face was, impossibly, one of confusion and sleep at the same time, as if she were suffering under some great inner turmoil, or had suddenly gone blind, but was not yet quite aware of it.

Jack Lutz had called to her repeatedly, of course, but it had become clear that she could not hear him, or *would* not hear him, so he had merely watched her.

He reached for her once, but his fingers went into her stomach without touching her, and that made him confused and fearful, so he did not try to do it again.

His lawyer had called just before Stevie's appearance in the living room. The police, his lawyer said, were on their way over to arrest Lutz in connection with Stevie's disappearance.

Lutz thought that when they arrived he would show them his wife, here, in the living room, and it would prove to them that she was *alive,* at least. He had no idea what might happen then.

"I'm sorry I hung up on you, Mr. Biergarten," Jenny Goodlow said at Ryerson's front door. She smiled an apology; Ryerson thought it was a very attractive and sincere smile, and he realized that in their two admittedly brief encounters, it was the first time he had seen it.

He stepped to one side, invited her into the town house, and led her to the living room, where he offered her a seat near the fireplace. She sat.

"Would you like a drink?" he asked.

"I don't drink," she said. "I used to, but not anymore." Another smile, this one a bit edgy.

Creosote pranced into the room and leaped into Ryerson's arms. It was a good jump, almost five feet, and Jenny Goodlow was apparently impressed.

"He certainly loves you, doesn't he, Mr. Biergarten," she said.

Ryerson asked her to call him Rye, she nodded, and he went on, "An ugly little dog, I know, but a real sweetheart."

Jenny nodded again, attempted another smile, but it did not work well. She shook her head, sighed. "Someone who said he was my brother came to see me."

Ryerson sat in a club chair nearby and put Creosote on the floor. "Was it a blond man? Tall, good-looking? Nicely trimmed beard?"

She shook her head. "No. This man was dark haired. Average height. He was good-looking, yes. But he had no beard. He looked . . . Mediterranean. Italian. He even had an accent. It wasn't an Italian accent; I've never heard an accent like it before." She shook her head again. Creosote came over and looked up at her. She grinned and tentatively touched the top of the dog's head.

"He doesn't bite," Ryerson said. "I don't think he *can* bite with that flat snout."

She scratched Creosote under the chin. She said, "This man wasn't my brother, of course. But he . . . knew things, Mr. Biergarten. You know, the kind of things that only brothers could know. It was very unnerving. I knew he wasn't my brother, of course, but I began to . . . doubt myself, I guess . . ."

Ryerson reached out, touched her hand. "Miss Goodlow," he began, but he had little idea how to continue. If he told her the truth—what he supposed was the truth, at any rate—she'd think he was nuts. He withdrew his hand. "Had you let this man into your house?"

She grimaced. "I'm not a fool. I talked to him through the screen door. It was just a short while ago, just before noon. He walked off, and he was gone. I called your number, got your housekeeper, learned that you'd stepped out for a while, and left a message with him that I was coming here. Actually, Mr. Biergarten, I'm a bit leery of going back to the house."

"I didn't get the message." He paused. "You could stay here, if you'd like."

She shook her head. "I'm booked into the Sheraton."

The boy thought that he was either being awfully brave or awfully stupid. Wasn't *he* the one who had decided that this strange mound of earth wasn't something to mess with? So what was he doing here, now, alone? Sometimes it was real difficult figuring himself out.

He poked at the mound with a long, thin stick. The dirt

seemed hard. Why not? he thought. It had settled overnight. He nodded to himself. Sure, the dirt had settled, so it was harder. And there had been a thunderstorm too, and wouldn't that make the dirt thicker?

No, it wouldn't, he realized. The rain would have washed some of the dirt away, and it wouldn't be *thicker,* there would be less of it.

So, it wasn't the *dirt* that was thicker and harder. He wasn't poking at the *dirt,* he was poking at something *in* the dirt.

A rock. Sure, he was poking at a big rock in the dirt.

He withdrew the stick, hesitated, took a step to his right, poked again. The stick sank into the dirt a few inches and stopped. He pushed. The stick sank no further into the dirt. He pushed harder. The stick snapped.

The noise of the stick snapping brought an *Ah!* of surprise from him. He stared wide-eyed at the mound for a moment, threw the stick down, turned, and ran home.

The big man knew that it had to be done and that he was the only one who could do it. He had brought this . . . thing up here in the first place—against the woman's wishes and, he had to admit, against her better judgment—and now it was up to him to dispose of it.

He stared at the body from twenty feet away. There was one dim overhead light on and in its soft, yellowish glow the body looked simply like one of the collectibles that had been stored up here for so long.

The big man held a fireplace poker tightly in his right hand. He had thought of using a gun on the little bastards that lived up here but had decided that that would be foolish—a slug could tear right through the floorboards and into the second floor of the house. Besides, he had always been leery of guns. Knives, clubs, and big cars were much more personal weapons, and that's the way he liked it when he killed—up close and personal.

He had a handkerchief over his mouth and nose, and because he was coming down with a head cold, it was difficult to breathe.

"Dammit!" he whispered into the handkerchief. This was something he definitely did not want to do. This was . . . offensive. Dirty. Bizarre. Grotesque. "Grotesque," he whispered, pleased with his choice of words. He thought that he had always been good with words.

He took a step forward. He stopped. The body seemed to be in motion and this sent a tremor of fear through him. He stared hard at the body and realized that it was not in motion, it only *looked* like it was in motion because the little bastards that lived up here were all over it, having their fill.

"Jesus!" whispered the big man, and turned and fled down the stairs to the second floor.

Sam Goodlow looked at his reflection in the window at his office and asked himself who he was seeing. That certainly wasn't *him*. That man was blond and handsome, and he oozed breeding and self-confidence. He—the real Sam Goodlow—oozed only clumsiness, bad taste, a sort of infantile vulnerability, and he always had.

And as he thought these things, his reflection changed and he was once again seeing a stocky, craggy-looking man with red hair and gentle gray eyes. Himself. The real Sam Goodlow. He was pleased. This latest "episode"—as he had come to think of them—had lasted quite a while.

Maybe he should see a shrink. What harm could it do? At worst, he'd simply get to know himself a little better, and that was always good for the soul.

He glanced at his desk, across the room. It was empty. *Empty?* he wondered. Why was his desk empty? This was his place of business and as long as he had conducted business here he had kept a good, cluttered desktop. Clients liked cluttered desks—it made them think he was busy, always on the move, that he didn't have time for something so mundane as neatness.

Except for clients like Violet McCartle. Classy old woman. "You're certainly not the neatest of men, are you, Mr. Goodlow?" she had said at their first meeting.

"Is it one of your requirements?"

She smiled. It was a good and gracious smile, but it looked to Sam as if it hurt. "I have a job for you, Mr. Goodlow. It's not much of a job, so I'm sure you can handle it." She produced a manilla envelope from her cavernous purse and handed it across the desk. The envelope was sealed and he began to open it. "No," she said. "Please don't. Not just yet."

"I don't understand."

"You will." She nodded to indicate the envelope. "My address is there. Could you please come and see me a week from today, about this time?"

"And don't look in the envelope?"

"No. But find a place to hide it, please. Find a very *good* place to hide it."

He wasn't sure. He liked having all the answers up front and this woman's cryptic way of doing business made him uneasy.

"I assure you," Violet McCartle said, "that all your questions will be answered a week from today.

He was still uncertain.

"There's a good deal of money in it for you, Mr. Goodlow."

This fact was not completely persuasive, but it helped.
"How much?" he asked.

"We'll settle that next week, okay?"

He thought a moment and said, "I'll be there."

"Good." She said nothing for a moment, then finished, "I look forward to seeing you." A quick, secretive smile flashed across her mouth.

The memory faded.

Sam looked at his reflection in the window again. He saw a craggy, red-haired man look back and he asked himself, "Is that me?"

SEVENTEEN

The old man's name was Fredrick and he was going into his cellar in search of his cat, Adam. Fredrick lived alone with Adam, and had for a long time.

Fredrick was going on eighty-five, Adam was going on nineteen, and the two made a happy if eccentric pair—one was almost continuously searching for the other because both were nearly blind and deaf, and both had a very hard time getting around.

It took Fredrick nearly five minutes to descend the short flight of stairs into his cellar. As he descended, he cast about for any sign of Adam, but saw only elongated lumps, vertical lumps, horizontal lumps, beige lumps, brown lumps, green lumps, all of which constituted part of the minutiae of his life—a dollhouse, a circa 1932 Lionel train set (all laid out on two ping-pong tables, but unused for decades), a floor lamp he and his wife had bought the day after coming home from their honeymoon, a lawn mower, hand-powered tools, a grandfather clock bearing a white patina of dust.

"Adam?" Fredrick called soothingly. "Come and have your dinner; it's time for dinner." Actually, it wasn't time for Adam's dinner—that time had come and gone several hours earlier and Fredrick hadn't noticed.

He carried a can of 9 Lives tuna supper with him. The can was unopened, but he believed that Adam could spot a can of 9 Lives tuna from a long way off and did not need to smell it. Adam's veterinarian told Fredrick that the cat was probably almost blind, and that his sense of smell was doubtless nearly gone, but Fredrick did not believe this. Adam was his companion, after all, and had been healthy all his life. Just like him.

Fredrick stopped to wonder if he had switched the light on in the cellar. He supposed that he had.

He turned and looked at the bare light bulb hanging from the rafters. It was switched on. This did not please him. He had hoped that he could add its light to the early morning light coming in the cellar windows.

He stepped forward. "Adam?" he called. "Come, come, Adam. Dinner time." There was no answering meow. He took another step forward. He was cautious here; the cellar was cluttered, and on his last visit he'd tripped over a can of paint and had nearly pitched headlong into the furnace.

He took another cautious step forward.

The air changed. It became cooler. He even supposed there was a little breeze.

"Adam?"

He smelled fish. *Fish?* he wondered. *In my cellar?* Perhaps he had fed Adam down here recently and what he was smelling was the cat food. But no—he always fed Adam in the kitchen. His long-term memory might be kaput, he thought, but his short-term memory was as good as a young man's.

He smelled salt air. *Fish, salt air?* he wondered.

And the tangy smell of earth. Wet clay.

He glanced about. The lumps in the basement seemed to have changed. He dug in his pants pockets for his glasses, found his keys, some change, then realized that he was wearing his glasses. "Dammit all!" he whispered.

One of the vertical lumps nearby moved. It was a lump as tall as a man and Fredrick leaned forward to get a better look at it. A white face and dark eyes appeared before him out of the fog of his near-blindness.

"Jesus Christ!" Fredrick screamed, and backed away from the face.

The vertical lump and the face vanished.

The air grew warmer.

He took another step backwards and reached out to push at the face that was no longer there. His heel hit the bottom stair, he fell backwards, and his arms flailed about. He caught the railing with his left arm, and sat down hard on the stair.

"What in the name of heaven . . ." he breathed.

After a few moments, he realized that he no longer smelled fish and salt air and wet clay.

He heard a meow at his feet. He looked. The orange lump that was Adam looked back.

Fredrick smiled, leaned over, and held his old cat close to him, as he would a baby.

As soon as he woke, early that same morning, Ryerson knew that Sam Goodlow was in the room. He couldn't see him; he didn't need to see him.

The room was dark and Ryerson noted Sam's predilection for coming to him in darkness. Perhaps the man did it for show.

Ryerson glanced about. "Hello," he said. "Sam?"

"Do you know what I am, Rye?" It was Sam's lazy tenor; it was nondirectional and it filled the room.

"Tell me what you are," Ryerson said.

"Puzzled. I'm puzzled. Befuddled. Benighted. No. No. Death didn't give me any answers, Rye. I expected answers. What did I get? Puzzled. Here I am, there I am. Half the time I don't know *who* I am or *where* I am, or even *that* I am, hell."

"I understand that," Ryerson said, and tried to think of something cogent to add. Nothing came to him.

"I think you're puzzled, too." It was a woman's voice, now.

"Perpetually, Sam."

"Was that a woman speaking? It's so hard to hear one's own voice—" Still the woman's voice.

"It's no problem, Sam. You're coming across just fine."

"I can see for you and be for you here, Ryerson."

"Sorry?"

"I think you need that." Sam's lazy tenor again. "I need you and you need me. You'll find my killer or you'll find me and I'll know what I am and where I am, and I'll find this lost woman who's married to the asshole and we'll both be as happy as rams."

"Clams, Sam?"

"As I said."

"Yes, I am puzzled, Sam. You say you don't know who killed you? I'd think that that would be easy for someone in your . . . position."

"Say that when you *are* in my position, Rye."

"You're right. I'm sorry."

"Perpetually puzzled and perpetually sorry. Who can operate at all well in an alien world? My killer lives and teethes in your world—"

"Lives and breathes, Sam?"

"Whatever. And the asshole's wife lives and breathes in

mine. And here we are, two detectives. Let's go and detect. I'll bash your head and you'll rub my feet."

"You mean, one hand will wash the other?"

"Which is what I said. Are you correcting me? Don't correct me. It's all I can do to stick here, hell. I'm being bugged, tugged all over, like taffy, Tom. I feel waffled, discerned, digested, muscled out and mutilated, and if my tense talk is in error, hell. I can see for you, and I can be for you, here, *you.* Yes or no? The heater's running."

"I understand."

"You wish you did."

"Of course. Yes."

"But you don't."

"I do, and I accept. Yes."

Silence.

"Sam?"

Nothing.

"Sam, are you still here?" He paused. "Are you still *here,* Sam?"

But Ryerson knew that he wasn't.

Fredrick's daughter was a tall, auburn-haired, and attractive woman of fifty-two whose name was Hanna Beckford. She came to look in on her father every couple of days, and although Fredrick knew that she thought of him as an invalid, and he resented her for it, he often looked forward to her visits. She was intelligent and had a droll sense of humor, much as had Fredrick's wife—Hanna's mother.

This morning, Hanna had found her father in the cellar babbling about "the face," and she was very concerned. She was even more concerned because he was cradling his cat in his arms, which he often did; but this morning, the cat was dead.

Hanna sat on the bottom cellar step, next to her father. She was trying to coax the dead cat from him, and she was trying, also, to find out what her father meant by "the face."

"Dad, I'm sorry, I'm so sorry," she told him, "but Adam is dead. Why don't you give him to me, Dad." And she put her hands on the dead cat, next to her father's hands.

But Fredrick protested, "He's sleeping, don't wake him, dammit!"

Hanna withdrew her hands.

"There's someone *down* here, you know!" Fredrick said.

Hanna shook her head. "Just you and me, Dad."

"And Adam. And the face."

"What face, Dad?"

Fredrick took one hand from the dead cat and pointed tremblingly toward the cellar wall. "There."

"That's just a wall."

"Dammit, I *know* it's a wall. I'm telling you that *someone* was standing in *front* of it." He idly scratched Adam behind the ears.

"Who?" asked Hanna.

"Who, who? Who knows who, for Pete's sake. Someone."

"And where is he now?"

"He? Did I say 'he'? I did not. It was a she."

"Oh."

"Oh? And what does that mean—'oh'? You think I'm having some geriatric sex fantasy, don't you, my girl? Well I'm not, and I *know* I'm not, because I know what geriatric sex fantasies are, I have them all the time, and this wasn't one of them."

Hanna sniffed. She smelled something odd. *Fish?* she wondered.

Fredrick said, "Smell that? Fish?"

"Do you feed the cat down here, Dad?"

"No, no, no. What a stupid suggestion. It takes me three hours to get down those damned stairs."

"But isn't that a can of cat food there?" Hanna nodded at the floor in front of Fredrick's feet. He leaned over a little, saw the can, said, "I was coaxing Adam with it."

Hanna smelled salt air. Wet clay. She glanced at the cellar windows—perhaps one was open and it was letting in salt air from the ocean six miles away. But the windows were closed.

She grew tense suddenly, as if someone were watching her. She turned her head, looked toward the big furnace. It was on the far side of the cellar, and it was lost in shadow.

"Dad, can you stand up?" She put a hand on Fredrick's elbow to coax him up.

"Smell that?" he said. "The ocean."

"Yes, I do. Stand up, Dad." She was becoming very tense, now.

"The ocean, Hanna. Down here in my cellar." He seemed oddly pleased.

"Stand up, dammit!"

He stood, shakily, and then looked as if he were going to fall. "Let go of the cat, Dad," Hanna told him. "The cat is dead."

He nodded. "I know." He stroked the cat lovingly. "I know he's not asleep, Hanna. I know he's dead. I'm going to bury him."

"That's good, Dad. Let's just get upstairs, okay."

He nodded again, but stayed put.

Hanna glanced quickly once more at the area of the furnace. The juxtaposition of furnace and shadow seemed to have changed. "Dad, move!"

"I'm trying to, Hanna. I can't."

"Of course you can. Just turn around and walk up the goddamned stairs."

"You do it, Hanna. I'm going to bury Adam."

"For God's sake, you can't bury him down here."

"But I can, Hanna." He smiled. It was a smile full of secret pleasure.

He moved forward, off the bottom step and toward the wall, where the face had appeared.

Hanna grabbed his arm.

He shook it away. "Leave me alone, girl!" The venom in his voice made his daughter step back. "Dad?" she pleaded.

He took another step toward the wall. Another. Another.

And he was gone.

"I'm surprised to see you, Rye," said Captain Bill Willis.

"I've had time to think things over," Ryerson said, "and I want to see if I can help." He nodded at Willis's desk. "Is that the file?"

Willis nodded and handed the file over. Ryerson opened it, looked through it quickly, closed it. "You don't seem to have added anything in the past week."

Willis shrugged. "It's not a high priority case, Rye. Legally, Sam Goodlow's simply a missing person, which is about as unique as athlete's foot."

Ryerson smiled, took some jelly beans from the open decanter on Willis's desk, and popped them into his mouth. He asked, as he chewed, "Can I take this?"—meaning the file on Sam Goodlow.

Willis shrugged again. "Sure. Just don't let anyone out there see you taking it, okay?" He nodded to indicate the big precinct room beyond his office.

"Okay," Ryerson said. He stood. "So you can't tell me

anything that's not here?" He tapped the file, which he held under his left arm.

Willis shook his head. "I'm hoping *you'll* be able to tell *us* something, Rye."

"I'll do what I can," Ryerson said.

EIGHTEEN

Rebecca Meechum had a key to Sam's office, and when she opened the door late that evening, she went immediately to the big window—it looked out on a railroad yard—and closed the wide, dark green shade, then the curtains. She felt very theatrical doing this, and it pleased her. Cloak-and-dagger stuff was fun.

After she'd closed the curtains, she turned on the desk lamp and opened the bottom right-hand drawer of the desk until it caught. She reached into the back of the drawer, then up, withdrew a manilla envelope lodged on the slats supporting the drawer above, put the envelope into her purse, and headed for the door.

"What's that?" she heard. She didn't recognize the voice. It was the voice of a man, and it was oddly accented.

She stiffened, halfway to the door.

"That envelope," the voice said. "What is it?"

She shook her head. "Nothing. Who are you?"

"Christ, who am I? Just tell me what's in the damned envelope, Becky."

"How do you know me?"

"How do I know you? How do I know you? Peels, don't sack my chin."

"Huh?"

"Like I said."

Rebecca turned her head. The desk lamp was still on, and in its yellow light, she could see that the small room was empty. Perhaps the man was in the bathroom. She looked at the bathroom door; it was closed. The closet, then. She looked. Its door was closed, too. "You're not there," she whispered.

"There, where," said the voice. "Don't yank my chain, Becky."

"Where are you?"

"Who knows, who knows. The envelope, please."

A form appeared behind the desk. It was as tall as a man and as indistinct as smoke.

Rebecca screamed, ran from the office and out to her car.

The form behind the desk muttered to itself, "Was it something I dead, I sighed? Something I lied? Something I said?"

Stevie Lutz had always loved the ocean. She'd swum in it, surfed in it, fished in it, sailed on it. She'd taken several ocean cruises to nowhere in particular. The destinations were not important; *being there,* on the ocean, was.

What she loved most about the ocean was it bigness. It was big in a way that even large lakes are not. An ocean's horizon stretches beyond itself.

She had always wanted to live in a house next to the ocean, but her husband had nixed that idea. The ocean made him queasy, he said. It was the smell of fish, he said. But she knew better. The ocean, so vast and so powerful, was beyond his control. And he *needed* to be in control.

This fact alone had, more than once, made her think about leaving him and finding someone else. But he had been her childhood sweetheart and they had always planned on being married. What an awful disappointment if all that planning and hope came to nothing. In that other life, it would be unbearable.

Here, it wasn't.

Because she had always loved the ocean.

And so she loved this place, created from the mist of her memory.

She was in control here.

She did not feel oppressed here. Or half alive.

Ryerson was walking Creosote on a well-lit street near his home. Creosote was not an easy dog to walk. He was too short, and the leash was too short, it was raining, and Creosote was reluctant to do his business in the rain, wanted to break out into a run, and could not. Ryerson had thought about getting a longer leash, a self-retracting fifteen-foot leash that would give the little dog some running room, but city ordinances did not allow such leashes, so Creosote had to be content to run in the town house.

A man was walking toward Ryerson. He was tall and stocky, was dressed in an overcoat and hat, and he made Ryerson feel suddenly tense. Ryerson could not see the man's face; the man's hat cast a shadow, but the man's gait—hands in his overcoat pockets, head down slightly, steps quick and short and purposeful—seemed threatening, and Ryerson stopped walking when the man was still fifty feet away.

The man stopped walking.

Creosote growled. It was more like a loud and ragged purr than a growl, and the man in the overcoat chuckled and called, "I'm sure he means well."

Ryerson didn't recognize the man's voice. It was deep, and accented, though he couldn't place the accent.

Ryerson said, "Do you have business with me?"

"I'm not sure."

"You don't know if you have business with me?"

"Is your name Sam Goodlow?"

"No."

"Then I don't have business with you."

"Why did you stop walking when I stopped walking?"

"I wasn't aware that I had."

"Yes, you did."

The man looked down at his feet. "You're right. I'm not walking."

Ryerson felt a moment of confusion. It was not his own confusion, he realized. It was the man's confusion. He was not what he appeared to be.

The man took his hands from his coat pockets. He shrugged, turned around, and walked back the way he had come, down the well-lit street, then, while Ryerson watched, turned left, down another street, and was gone.

Moments later, a car appeared from the street the man had turned on. The car was big and important looking, but Ryerson was lousy with makes of cars and so could not say what kind it was. It turned away from Ryerson; he heard the hum of its big engine, noted the car's license number—a vanity plate; it read BIG MAMA—and then, in a split second, the car was gone, as if the rainy night had swallowed it up.

Ryerson glanced at Creosote, who glanced back, flat face a blank. Ryerson said, "What the hell was *that* all about, do you think?" Had the man really been on the street? Ryerson wondered. Or the car?

But Creosote wasn't talking.

*   *   *

Ryerson was on the phone with Captain Bill Willis minutes later. "I need you to check out a license plate number for me, Bill."

"Sure. What is it?"

"Massachusetts, I think; B-I-G," he spelled, "space, M-A-M-A."

" 'BIG MAMA'?"

" 'BIG MAMA.' "

"Okay. The Motor Vehicle Department's closed now, of course, but I'll call you tomorrow morning."

The man's wife had been dead for ten years, but he still missed her terribly. He missed her so much, in fact, that he hadn't dated anyone in the decade since her death, although he was a good-looking man and had had many offers.

He dreamt of her often. He dreamt of their brief time together, of their lovemaking—which had been nothing short of spiritual—of their quiet moments, their public hand-holding and caressing, their wordless conversations, the kinds of conversations that only two very alike people can have.

He missed all of her. He missed her little flirtatious glances, her quick and musical laughter, her defiant sort of walk, her breasts, her hands—though two of her fingers were gnarled by early arthritis—her eyes that told him just how well she knew him, and how happy that made her.

He had longed a thousand times for her to come to him after her death. He would have easily accepted the corruption of her body, because he knew that her spirit was incorruptible.

And he was very grateful when she did come to him, at last, and she was whole and flirtatious and sexual and uncorrupted.

She lifted the blankets and slipped in beside him, fondled him, stroked him.

He was ready within the moment, and she straddled him in the semidarkness.

He whispered her name.

But she did not whisper his. She was lost in her grinning and loose-armed pleasure. She had always been the acrobat, had always given him such delicious pain.

He whispered her name again, hoping now for recognition from her.

"Jack!" she whispered back, and though it sounded oddly angry, he smiled, because his name was Jack. But it was not *his* name she had whispered, and he did not know it.

Soon, she left him.

NINETEEN

At 9:30 the following morning, Captain Willis called Ryerson to tell him that BIG MAMA was registered to a woman named Violet McCartle, and gave Ryerson the woman's address.

It was in Boston's Back Bay section. The house that belonged to Violet McCartle was huge and ostentatious; blue painted stone lions guarded the front gates. So did a large man in a black uniform who bent way over to talk to Ryerson through the Woody's open driver's window.

"Do you have an appointment, sir?"

"No," Ryerson answered.

"Then you aren't getting in, I'm sorry."

"Perhaps you could call Mrs. McCartle and leave my name."

"I can do that," said the large man. "What's your name?"

"Sam Goodlow."

"Okay. Wait here." The man called the woman in the house and came back to the car. "Go ahead, Mr. Goodlow," he said, and as he said this, the tall iron gates swung open.

* * *

A thin, sixtyish woman stood at the front door of the house. The woman was wearing a gray dress, no shoes, and her demeanor spoke clearly of impatience.

As Ryerson came up the long flight of stone steps, she shouted at him—her voice was like the call of a crow—"I'm Violet McCartle. Who are you?"

"I'm Sam Goodlow," Ryerson called back. He noted the recently erected wooden ramp to the left of the steps. It was clearly designed to accommodate a wheelchair.

"No, you aren't Sam Goodlow," the woman shouted. "Tell me who you are."

Ryerson did not answer immediately. He sensed that she would allow him to come all the way up the steps before she alerted the man at the gates.

Ryerson reached the top step and offered his hand. She glanced at it and repeated, "You aren't Sam Goodlow. Tell me who you are or I'll have you ejected at once."

Ryerson let his hand drop. "My name's Ryerson Biergarten," he said. "I'm a friend of Sam Goodlow's."

"No. I don't think so."

Ryerson sensed uncertainty from her. Her eyes were faded blue and canny and she looked like she could be a formidable opponent, despite her frail appearance. Her voice, now that she wasn't shouting, was strong and commanding. If he hadn't been who he was—if he had had to depend solely on his five senses—he would have assumed without question that she knew him to be a liar.

Ryerson said, "Sam and I met shortly before his disappearance, Mrs. McCartle. He told me about you."

"Did he?" Less uncertainty. She grinned. Her teeth were straight and white; Ryerson supposed they were her own. "And what was it that he told you?"

"Of your relationship."

"That sounds smarmy, Mr. Biergarten. Was it meant to sound smarmy?"

Ryerson shook his head. "I'm sorry, no. I meant your business relationship."

Her grin drooped, then returned, wider. "You're fishing, Mr. Biergarten. I can feel it. You may know Mr. Goodlow, you may know *of* him, but I doubt you're his friend." She stepped back and put her hand on the door to close it.

Ryerson stepped forward, put his hand on the doorknob, and said, "You live here alone, isn't that true?" He knew it was true; he had read it from her.

She glared at his hand on the doorknob. "Mr. Biergarten, you are perilously close to having your testicles squashed."

The phrase surprised him—she had said it with such venom and sincerity. He let go of the doorknob and said, as she closed the door, "Sam told me that you hired him." He sensed something strange about the woman, something he couldn't pinpoint.

She closed the door. It was made of glass, with iron scrollwork, and he could see her peer out at him a moment, turn, and move off into the bowels of the house.

Ryerson asked himself, *Who is she? She isn't Violet Mc-Cartle.* He had little idea how he knew this. He'd never met Violet McCartle.

He leaned forward, put his face to the door to peer into the house.

He saw the woman looking back at him from the far end of the long hallway.

Moments later, he sensed that someone was behind him, at the bottom of the long flight of steps. He looked. The giant of a man who had been guarding the front gates was there. His face was blank. He stood very tall and very straight, and he needed to say nothing.

Half a minute later, Ryerson was in the Woody and on his way back to the town house.

Sam Goodlow was in the car with him. "Who was that?" he asked from the third seat.

Ryerson had sensed Sam's presence only a moment before Sam had spoken, so Sam's question gave him a start. He missed a stop sign and a car coming through the intersection braked hard, its horn blared, a volley of curses filled the air.

"Watch what you're doing," Sam warned.

"Don't take me by surprise."

"You think I can help it?"

Ryerson sighed and glanced in the rearview mirror, first at Sam—who was as Ryerson remembered, multicolored insides and grinning outsides, and then at the driver he'd cut off, who was, thankfully, turning the other way.

"So, who was that?" Sam repeated.

"You don't know?" Ryerson asked.

"Would I ask if I knew?"

Ryerson shook his head. "She says her name is Violet McCartle. Does that ring a bell?"

"It doesn't ring a thing."

"You know, Sam, you're talking better."

"Am I? I get lots of rest. A body needs rest."

Ryerson grinned. "Was that a joke?"

"It could have been. I don't know. I have something for you; I know where the asshole's wife is."

Silence.

"And?" Ryerson coaxed.

"My God, my God, that lady back there threatened to

squash your testicles! That's a horrible thing. I cannot see a sweet old lady squashing someone's testicles. It's ludicrous, obscene, it galls the eyeballs, I can barely stand to rehash it, but there it is."

"Could we stick to the subject, Sam?"

"I don't know, I don't know. The subject keeps changing, especially from where I sit. You'll see, when it's your turn in the backseat. First, *this* is the subject, then *that* is the subject, and sometimes there are multiple subjects within a given moment, and *there* the moments are, all laid out like the trails of snails, time elongated, stretched, pulled and postulated, and you know, you know, there are no moments unless we're beyond them."

Silence.

Ryerson said, "End of speech?"

"The asshole's wife is all divided, Rye, and they're using her soul for fun and games and auld lang syne. The poor thing is as lost as a penny and she doesn't even know it."

"Sam, you're going to have to be a bit more specific; you're speaking in riddles."

"It's kind of a Zen thing."

"Sorry?"

"Memories are made of these, Rye."

Silence.

Ryerson glanced in the rearview mirror.

Sam was gone.

The woman who called herself Violet McCartle said to the big man, "You are very good at what you do. And I pay you well for it."

"You're talking about the guy who just left, am I correct?"

"Yes. Ryerson Biergarten. I've heard of him. He's a psychic. And my guess is, he's legitimate. He could spell real trouble for me—"

"Yes, I know."

"Don't interrupt. It's discourteous. I want you to find out, first, what he knows about our friend, what he knows, or *thinks* he knows, about Violet, then bring the information back to me."

"I assume you want him dead?"

"And I assume that that was a rhetorical question. Eventually, he will have to die, of course. But we must be careful about the web we're weaving here. We might be increasing our troubles geometrically. You will do nothing without consulting me first, although I'm sure you understand that without my having to say it."

"As a matter of fact, yes."

The woman smiled. "You really are a smart ass son of a bitch underneath that gruff exterior, aren't you?"

"And I assume that *that* was a rhetorical question."

"No, it was an observation. Now, go and do as I've asked."

TWENTY

The boys could not find their way back to the strange mound in the woods, although they had been looking for hours, following paths they were sure they recognized, passing landmarks that seemed familiar. But one path through the woods looks much the same as another, and landmarks—fence posts, gnarled trees, stumps—turn out to be less than unique. So the boys were becoming frustrated, angry, and tired.

The first boy—who had been to the mound only once—complained that the mosquitoes would soon be out in droves, and the second boy protested that the mosquitoes came out at dusk, which was still a couple of hours off.

"What we should do," the first boy suggested, "is go back home and *tell* someone. You know, like a cop."

"And you know what would happen if we did that?" countered the second boy. "The cop would ask us why we didn't say anything the first time we were here, and we'd get in lots of trouble. Witholding evidence, it's called. What's the matter, you don't watch TV?"

"I watch as much TV as you do and you know it."

They walked while they were talking, which was the way of adolescents—mouths and feet always moved.

And as they talked, they found themselves at the spot they'd been looking for. The first boy, who was taller and stockier than the second, saw it first, and he put his hand out against the second boy's stomach to stop him. "Here it is."

"Yeah," breathed the second boy, as if awestruck.

"What do we do now?"

The second boy didn't answer right away.

"Well?" coaxed the first boy.

"Dig it up, I guess."

"Yeah, that's what we gotta do, huh?"

"Yeah."

Jack Lutz was upset. "I'm calling you from the damn jail, Mr. Biergarten. They've locked me up, for Christ's sake. They think I murdered Stevie. I showed her to them when they came to pick me up. She was *there*, Mr. Biergarten. She was in the house. And I showed her to them. I said, 'There she is.' But they didn't see her, and then *I* didn't see her either. She was gone. Again. And then they brought me here.

"Now, I know you've got some influence with these people, I know they listen to you, so I want you to do what you can to convince them I'm telling the truth."

Ryerson sighed.

"Mr. Biergarten, please don't say no. Have you ever been in jail? It's not a nice place. It smells of urine. It smells of *piss*. And you know why? Because people *pee* in here. Did you know that, Mr. Biergarten? People pee in their cells."

"I'll do what I can, Mr. Lutz, but I really can't promise that my intervention will—"

"Oh, fuck. Just tell them you saw her—"

"But I didn't see her."

"I know that. Aren't you *listening* to me. I'm suggesting a way out of this . . ."

And while Ryerson and Jack Lutz were talking, the two boys were digging. They dug very slowly, as if they were part of an archaeological expedition—one small spoonful at a time. There was no other way. They supposed that their parents would think it was odd if they brought shovels out here, so they brought soup spoons, instead, which were easily concealed.

And they dug slowly, too, because they were certain of what they'd find, and they were not at all sure they wanted to find it.

The smaller boy was the first to notice the smell. "Jeez, smell that? It smells like shit."

"Skunk cabbage," nodded the larger boy. "Ain'tcha ever smelled it before? Awful, huh?"

"I smelled skunk cabbage before, and this ain't skunk cabbage."

"What else can it be?"

The smaller boy straightened from his digging and nodded grimly at the mound of earth. "It could be whatever's in there and you know it."

The larger boy straightened. Imagining what might be in the mound of earth was one thing, but actually *smelling* it was another matter entirely.

They stared silently at the mound of earth for a long while. And as they stared, the smell from within the mound grew stronger, until the smaller boy supposed that he could actually *taste* it, the way he could taste the smell of gasoline when his father filled up the car and the gas spilled over onto the bumper.

He—the smaller boy—was the first to break the silence.

"Ever seen a dead body before?" he whispered, and he put his hand over his mouth and nose.

The larger boy nodded slightly. "My grandmother. She was sitting up in her chair and she was dead. We found her on Christmas Eve."

"That's really awful."

The larger boy shrugged. "Nah. She just looked like she was sleeping." He nodded at the mound of earth. "Whoever's in there ain't gonna look like they're sleeping, though."

"Damn right."

"Damn right I'm damned right."

A moment later, some of the earth covering the mound gave way, revealing a gray hand within. The hand was long fingered, slender. It wore a thin gold wedding ring.

"Shit!" whispered the larger boy.

"A hand," whispered the smaller boy. "It's a woman in there." But he was speaking to no one. His friend had already turned and run for home.

"And you were in that hunter's cabin, too," Jack Lutz protested. "So you know I'm not lying. I mean, you *know* I'm not lying."

"I suspect as much, at any rate, Mr. Lutz," Ryerson said. "But what I suspect is not going to carry a lot of weight with the Boston PD."

"Don't give me that. You're just trying to weasel out of your responsibilities to me."

"Mr. Lutz, I'll call Captain Willis and talk to him. It's all I can do."

"Thanks for nothing," Lutz said, and hung up.

* * *

Fredrick—the octogenarian who had disappeared into his cellar wall—knew where he was and he wasn't sure that he liked it very much. There was his cat, Adam, trotting ahead of him through the mist, looking back every now and then to give his human a summoning meow.

And there, around him, suspended in the mist, was the bric-a-brac of his past—houses he had lived in, friends and lovers who had left him years ago, animals he had owned, especially memorable moments from his long life.

And he thought that all of this was well and good, and very tempting, too—that if he were not who he was, then he would probably stay here, and literally be as happy as he had ever been, forever.

But all of this would come his way sooner or later, anyway. After he had come to it legitimately. In ten years or so, when his body finally gave up the ghost.

For now, this place was simply annoying because there was no *reason* for him to be here now, and every reason to be back where he had come from, with his daughter, Hanna, who loved him, and with his surviving friends, who were numerous.

And Adam—trotting far ahead and giving him a summoning meow every now and then—would wait.

TWENTY-ONE

I 've got a joke," said Sam Goodlow. "How many spooks does it take to screw in a light bulb?"

Ryerson thought about this a moment and said, "I give up. How many spooks does it take to screw in a light bulb?"

"None. Spooks can't screw. They're dead."

Ryerson forced a chuckle. "That's pretty grim, Sam."

They were in Ryerson's office. Ryerson was seated behind his desk.

"Yeah," Sam said. "Grim."

"Do you know that I can't see you?" Ryerson said.

"Nor I you," Sam said. "I see the furniture. I see your desk, the windows, the chair." He paused. "I called you. I remember that."

The abrupt change of subject took Ryerson by surprise. "When?" he asked.

"Before . . . this."

"You mean before you died?"

"If it's what you want to believe, Rye, though I think the jury is still out on that matter."

A thin white line appeared in the far corner of the office.

It widened slowly. These words came from it: "Now I see. There you are."

"And there you are," Ryerson said.

The smaller boy had found himself transfixed by the hand in the dirt. Unlike his friend—who'd run off minutes earlier—he'd never seen a dead person, and here, right in front of him, was a dead hand and arm. Here was a wedding ring, long red fingernails, wrinkled gray skin. A *woman* was attached to all that. The woman was in the dirt.

And that dirt probably clogged her mouth. She couldn't scream if she wanted to. And she couldn't see, or smell, or touch. She could touch only the dirt, and see only the dirt, and smell only herself. And she could think only about the dirt. She couldn't think about anything else because the dirt was all over her and inside her, probably. All she had was the dirt. She *was* the dirt and the dirt was her.

The boy wanted to move forward and uncover her, *see* her, see the face under the dirt. He wanted to find out if all the horror movies were correct, if the dead and buried really *looked* dead and buried.

But he was transfixed and paralyzed by fear and indecision. He could hear his pulse in his ears, he could hear his quick breathing, and he knew dimly that he had his hand cupped over his mouth and nose to keep out the smell of the thing in the dirt, the woman in the dirt.

And he realized dimly, too, that he was weeping.

He knew also that he wanted to see the woman's face because then she would stop being the nightmare she was now—a wrinkled, gray, and smelly thing in the dirt. If he could see her face, she would become human. She would become only a poor, dead woman in the dirt.

He thought that he took a step toward her.

And another.

It was some other boy moving, not himself.

Another step.

Then he was bending over, toward the thing in the dirt. He could see his hand, the soup spoon clutched in it. He could see the spoon penetrate the dirt, could see the spoon come away with its little burden.

He threw the dirt over his shoulder, came forward with the spoon again, got some more dirt, threw it, came forward, got more dirt, threw it. This was slow motion, fast motion, no motion. This was some other boy's spoon, some other boy's arm.

Then he could see hair beneath the dirt. Gray hair, white hair, blond hair. Who knew? It was matted with dirt. And then a smooth gray forehead appeared, and thin white eyebrows.

Then eyes were revealed beneath the dirt, and they were closed, and the boy sighed through his weeping.

A nose appeared—long, and straight, nostrils flared forever.

Gray, hollow cheeks and wide, gray mouth. Puckered lips. Full, puckered, gray lips.

Kiss, kiss.

Sam Goodlow was seated in a big, winged-back chair across from Ryerson's desk. He was resting his head against the back of the chair and was wearing a rumpled gray suit. He looked comfortable.

He also looked oddly damp.

Ryerson asked him why, but Sam couldn't say. "I've been like this for a while," he explained, and lifted his arm as if to look at the sleeve of his rumpled suit. "Am I wearing anything?" he asked.

"Yes, a suit," Ryerson answered.

"Sure," Sam said, "a suit," and he let his arm fall and rested his head against the back of the chair again. "How are memories and minestrone alike?" he asked.

Ryerson said, "I don't know."

"They are, that's all," Sam explained drily. "My memories are like soup. Minestrone, chowder. Name your soup. No clear soups. Only unclear."

"Yes," Ryerson said. "I understand."

"No you don't, you don't. Who could, or won't? Tell me I'm not alive, Rye. I won't believe you. I *am* alive."

On the street below, the big man looked up at the window behind which Ryerson and Sam were talking and he thought that he really couldn't wait to have a chance at killing again. If anything was good in his life, it was the killing he did—that manipulation, that control! Nothing was as simple or as everlasting as the extinction of a life, a psyche, a soul. One slow movement of the foot on the gas pedal, steady hands on the steering wheel, that so-satisfying *whump!* and a life that had been, suddenly wasn't!

He sighed and lit up a cigarette.

"You're always changing," Ryerson said to Sam Goodlow.

"I'm just trying to find my equilibrium," Sam said from his winged-back chair. "Just trying to find the point of rest."

Creosote sauntered in, hopped up on Ryerson's lap, and looked blankly at Sam Goodlow, who said, "I never had a dog. I wanted a dog. You have a dog."

"Yes," Ryerson said, "I have a dog." He became uneasy. When the conversation started meandering like this, it usually meant that Sam was drifting off. Ryerson went on, "Who did you talk to when you called?"

"A man who sneezed."

"You mean he sneezed while you were talking to him? Was his name Matthew?"

Sam did not look at Ryerson. He kept his head on the back of the chair and said, "He answered the phone, I talked to him, he sneezed. That's all there is to it."

"My housekeeper and I are the only ones here, Sam. So you had to have talked to him."

"Memories are made of sneeze."

Ryerson sighed. Creosote gurgled.

"*Did* you talk to him, Sam?"

"He sneezed, I hung up, I died, I cried, I lied."

Sam's rumpled, damp suit began to fade. His body appeared. He was white and stocky and hairy. He said, "And now I'm naked, right?"

"It's not something you can control, is it?" Ryerson asked.

"I *am* controlled," Sam answered.

Then his bones appeared, and his insides, and the chair was empty.

Janice Erb said over the phone to the woman who called herself Violet McCartle, "You know, of course, that you've sustained a terrific loss selling your portfolio at this time. And I might add that—as I predicted—there has been a measurable effect on the market itself."

"No pain, no gain," said the woman known as Violet McCartle. "I assume you've transferred the funds as I requested."

"Of course."

"Then our relationship is at an end."

"Regretfully, yes. Let me know when I can be of service to you again, Mrs. McCartle."

"Of course, Ms. Erb."

TWENTY-TWO

I'm looking at her right now," the man said. He was calling the police from a phone booth on the corner of Joseph and Fitzhugh Streets, in North Boston. "She's not more than ten feet away," the man continued, "and I tell you, she's crazy. Someone's got to come and pick her up."

"When you say she's crazy, sir," asked the desk sergeant on the other end of the line, "what exactly do you mean? Is she threatening anyone?"

"What I mean is, she's calling out this guy's name over and over again."

"And what name is that?"

"Jack. She's saying Jack over and over again, like a crazy person, and I tried to talk to her but she acted like I wasn't even there, like she could see through me, so I thought I'd better call you guys."

"Could you describe the woman, please?"

"Sure. She's tall, she's got long brown hair, she's thin."

"And what is the woman wearing?"

"A wedding dress."

"This woman is wearing a wedding dress?"

"Yes. And it looks very old and very dirty. That's one of the reasons I called you. I mean, it's bad enough that she's calling out this guy's name and doesn't respond to anyone, but she's wearing this god-awful wedding dress, too—"

"Give me your location, sir, and we'll dispatch a car at once."

"She's gone."

"Gone?"

"Just like that. My God. She simply vanished, pfft! Into nothing."

Rebecca Meechum thought that she was the soul of restraint. For three days now, she'd had that envelope and she hadn't opened it. She had held it up to the light, had even begun to steam it open, but had quickly decided that she would be found out, and so had abandoned the effort.

She wished the woman would come and pick up the envelope, as she had said she would. Didn't the woman know what a temptation it was, didn't she realize that by telling her—Rebecca—not to open the envelope that that was precisely what she would be driven to do?

It was as if the woman was . . . perverse, or something. As if she *knew* that Rebecca would have to do the thing she had been told not to and then she—the woman—would relish making her—Rebecca—suffer the consequences.

But what could the consequences be, after all? The woman had made no threat, she had simply said, "Do not open the envelope. Wait for me to pick it up." There was no threat in that. Not even an implied threat.

Rebecca held the large manilla envelope up to the bright daylight coming in through her bedroom window. She saw only a rectangular dark shadow in the envelope that was a little smaller than the envelope itself.

Photograph, she decided. It wasn't the first time she'd thought that it was what the envelope contained. It was obvious. The thing in the envelope was opaque. Regular paper would have let some light through, at any rate. Thick photographic paper probably wouldn't. It didn't take a modern-day Sherlock Holmes to figure that out.

Her doorbell rang.

Sam remembered this:

"Hello again, Mr. Goodlow. Come in, please."

"Hello, Mrs. McCartle."

"Please. Violet."

"Sure." He went into the big, ostentatious house and followed the woman down a long hallway, into a cavernous room filled with antiques.

She sat.

He sat nearby.

"So, tell me what you've done with the envelope, Mr. Goodlow."

He hesitated, uncertain. Something about the woman puzzled him. He studied her a moment. Canny, gray-blue eyes; short, white hair; strong, rectangular face.

"Mr. Goodlow?" the woman coaxed.

Perhaps, he thought, the key to what puzzled him lay in her voice. It was not precisely the voice he remembered, though he wondered how good his memory could be after a week, and after such a brief conversation.

"Mr. Goodlow? The envelope?"

"Sure," he said. "It's at my office. It's hidden in the overhead lighting fixture."

"You'll have to do better than that, Mr. Goodlow." The voice came from behind him, in the doorway, and it was nearly identical to the voice of the woman seated in front of him.

He turned, looked.

* * *

Ever since her father's disappearance, Hanna Beckford had not left his house. More than once, she had lifted the telephone receiver after deciding that she needed to call *someone*. But she had called no one because it came to her that what she had to say—*My father walked into the cellar wall and disappeared!*—was impossible, and she would be looked upon as a crazy person.

So she had waited for him.

She was certain that if he could indeed disappear into a cellar wall, then he could very well reappear from the same wall, and when he did, he would need her to be there, because who knew where he might have gone, who knew the trauma he might have suffered?

He would need her. And she would have to be there for him.

She spent most of her time in her father's kitchen. The cellarway was off the kitchen, and she kept the door open. She had brought a cot into the kitchen, and a TV, which she watched with the sound turned off so she wouldn't miss hearing the reappearance of her father.

It frightened her to stay in her father's house. She remembered the presence she had sensed in the far corner of the cellar just moments before her father's disappearance, and though she had tried to convince herself that she had sensed nothing but what her own nervousness had manufactured, she did not believe it. She had been within spitting distance of something powerful enough to whisk her father away as if he had never existed, and she was very fearful of it, so fearful that she had lain awake now for three nights.

But her fear was not as great as the love she had for her father, so she had waited at his kitchen table, had played endless rounds of losing solitaire, and had watched her father's old TV show her faint gray and white images of the colorful and tacky and predictable world that existed beyond his big, empty house.

And she had waited for him to reappear.

When, at last, he did, she was not prepared for it.

She had thrown down a king of hearts as unuseable, had glanced toward the cellarway, to her right, thinking she had heard a noise from below. But it was not the first noise she had heard. The house was home to several families of mice, and they were not quiet.

And when she looked at her hand of solitaire again, and thought dimly that she was again going to lose, but that it didn't much matter, she felt a strong hand on her shoulder, and she heard, "What a strange and wonderful universe we live in, Hanna. Who could have known?"

And Sam remembered saying, as he stared at the woman in the doorway, "What the hell is *this* all about? What are you, twins?"

The woman in the doorway smiled a little, as if at a private joke. She was sitting very erect in a wheelchair, as if she were unaccustomed to sitting in it. "No, Mr. Good-low," she said. "But we might as well be twins, as you can see."

Sam looked at the other woman for a moment, then looked again at the woman in the doorway. "Is this some kind of scam you're running?"

The woman shook her head. "No scam, Mr. Goodlow. Just good business sense. Violet McCartle has need of a twin at this point in her life. Actually, what she has need of is not a twin, but a double. Someone that the world— especially the shark-infested world of business—will believe is her. The strong prey on the weak, we all know that, don't we, Mr. Goodlow? So sometimes a little sleight of hand is required."

"And you're the double?" he asked the woman.

She smiled, again as if at a private joke. And the other woman said, "Your understanding of this whole affair must remain, necessarily, quite limited."

He looked from one face to the other. "So what you're saying is that you're not going to tell me which one of you is the real Violet McCartle, right?" He grinned. "It's an interesting game, but it's not going to work." He looked at the woman on the settee. "You visited me at my office last week, Mrs. McCartle. I remember your voice."

She nodded. "Yes, Mr. Goodlow. *Someone* did indeed visit you."

He thought about this a moment, then whispered a curse.

The other woman said, "And I would have to reiterate, Mr. Goodlow, that your overhead lighting fixture is not really the best or the most secure of places for the envelope that was entrusted to you."

"Perhaps a safe-deposit box," said the woman on the settee.

Sam shook his head. "This isn't going any further until I know precisely who I'm talking to."

A moment's silence followed, then the woman on the settee said, "Violet McCartle will call you tomorrow at precisely 5:30 P.M. Please be available." She leaned forward and handed a small business envelope to Sam. He opened it. It contained a check for twenty thousand dollars.

Sam looked at the check for a couple of seconds, then nodded and said, "Sure. I'll be there."

TWENTY-THREE

The homicide detective hadn't doubted that the boys had found what they claimed to have found, but, after following them through the thick woods for two hours, he had strongly doubted that they'd be able to lead him to their discovery.

But then they were there, at the mound. The detective could see the gray arm, the gray face, the full, puckered lips, and matted hair, and, nearly in a panic—as if the boys would be forever scarred by viewing this obscenity longer than they already had—he pushed them away, turned them around, and approached the mound very cautiously.

Matthew Peters came to Ryerson's office door and announced another visitor.

"Did you get a name?" Ryerson asked.

Matthew shook his head. Ryerson sighed. Matthew said, "It's a kid. A little boy. He says it's urgent."

Ryerson's brow furrowed in confusion. "Really?" he said, more to himself than to Matthew, who said, "Shall I show him into the living room, Mr. Biergarten?"

"Yes. I'll be right down," Ryerson answered.

* * *

The boy was in his early teens, Ryerson guessed, thin, red haired, with a splash of freckles across his nose. He was wearing blue jeans and a red flannel shirt. His feet were bare, which surprised Ryerson. The boy looked very Huck Finn–ish. He was standing at one of two tall, narrow windows that looked out on Market Street. His hands were in his jeans pockets and though he was clearly trying to look casual, he looked very nervous.

He said, as Ryerson came up to him and offered his hand, "You are Mr. Biergarten?"

"I am."

The boy shook Ryerson's hand. Ryerson noted that the boy's skin was unusually cool and dry, although his grip was very firm.

"I have a job for you, Mr. Biergarten," the boy said.

"Do you really?" Ryerson noted the patronizing tone in his voice and regretted it. He saw that the boy apparently noticed it too, because he frowned and looked away, then looked back quickly. "Yes," he said firmly, "I do. And I can pay you, too."

Ryerson gestured at a pair of club chairs nearby. "Why don't we sit down and discuss it."

The boy shook his head. "No. I don't need to sit down. I like it here."

"At the window?"

The boy nodded. "Lots of daylight," he said, and smiled coyly.

Ryerson grew uncomfortable. He was beginning to sense something odd about this boy, something false. He looked at the boy's bare feet and asked, "What happened to your shoes?"

"Don't need 'em." Another coy smile.

"I see."

"Who needs shoes except people who are goin' some-where?"

Ryerson shrugged. "Good question," he said.

"Damn straight."

Several seconds of tense silence followed. The boy's un-blinking green eyes would not leave Ryerson, and Ryer-son's uneasiness grew.

"Could you tell me your name?" Ryerson asked.

The boy nodded but did not answer.

Ryerson grinned weakly. "And your name is . . ."

"Sam."

Ryerson nodded and said, "Sam Goodlow?"

"The same."

Ryerson sighed.

The boy said, "And I have a job for you. There's a man following me. A great big man. Bigger than you. Wider, anyway. And he makes me very scared, and I need you to help me."

"Why don't we sit down?"

"I don't need to sit down. I don't need to sit down or wear shoes or do anything. And you *have* to help me."

The thin, gray-haired woman in Rebecca Meechum's apart-ment smiled playfully. "You're not really going to try and make me believe that you did not look in this envelope, are you, Miss Meechum?"

The woman had a large, black leather purse slung over her right arm. The purse was bulky, and as the woman talked, her hand went into it.

Rebecca Meechum had already handed the manilla enve-lope over and the woman was clutching it in her free hand. She had not opened it; apparently, she knew what was inside and did not need to open it.

Rebecca smiled nervously, her gaze alternating between the woman's playful gray-blue eyes and the big, bulky purse. "I wanted to open it," Rebecca said. "I mean, who wouldn't? You tell someone not to do something, and that's precisely what they're going to want to do."

"Certainly," said the woman, and her playful smile broadened a bit. "It makes perfect sense. And I think that I may even believe that you did not look in the envelope. It makes no difference whatever if you did or didn't. We hired you to become involved with Mr. Goodlow for a reason, of course. And now that he has, as they say, gone the way of the dinosaurs, your usefulness has come to an abrupt end." She withdrew a small-calibre pistol from her purse and pointed it at Rebecca's head.

Rebecca held her hands up, palms out, at chest level. "You really don't have to do this," she pleaded. "Honest."

"Oh," said the woman, "but I really do. And I'll tell you why." Her smile grew flat and merciless. "Because I *like* it." And she fired.

Halfway up the stairs to his office, the young, red-headed boy behind him, Ryerson had looked back and seen the boy give way to the man.

And now, Ryerson could see him as a whole person. He wondered if it was how Sam could see himself. He asked, "How do you see yourself, Sam?"

"As a lost soul, Ryerson," Sam answered.

"Oh."

"But that was neither the extent or the intent of your question, was it?"

"It suffices."

"Some say the world will end in fire," Sam intoned, "others say in ice. But from what I know of desire, I hold with those who favor fire, though ice is nice, and will suffice." He smiled. It was the biggest, most self-satisfied and toothy smile that Ryerson had ever seen.

"Robert Frost," he said.

"Is it?" Sam said. "It just came to me, as if someone were whispering in my ear. Who reads anymore?" His smile flickered and was gone. "His name was Matthew, yes, I remember, it returns, echoes, recapitulates, rehashes. Matthew. He who sneezes."

"You talked to him on the phone?"

"Yes."

"And you gave him some message? Do you remember the message, Sam?"

Sam shook his head. He looked miserable. He said, his gaze on the ceiling, his big hands flat on the arms of the winged-back chair, "People are beginning to whisper to me, Ryerson. They're whispering to me right now, even as I speak, even as I . . . listen, listen, I hear them, little, anonymous whispers, like the sounds of children playing in closed rooms. Ryerson, who *knows* what message I gave? Can I speak, can I tell?"

"Don't fade away just now, Sam—"

"Ask a cloud not to evaporate, a breeze not to die, a memory not to be lost, Ryerson, listen, listen, listen, hear them? Hear them? The whispers! It is all poetry, anonymous poetry, like the comingled songs of morning birds . . . Oh, God, God, this is so very embarrassing, to wax rhapsodic about . . . about heaven. Matthew, yes, I gave him a message, I told him this."

Silence.

"Told him what?" Ryerson asked.

"I sing the body electric—"

Silence.

"You're reciting poetry, Sam."

"It's kind of a Zen thing."

"Matthew?" Ryerson coaxed.

" 'I need to speak with Ryerson Biergarten,' I said. 'Do I have the right number?'

"And Matthew said, 'Yes, this is the Biergarten residence. My name is Matthew. I'm Mr. Biergarten's assistant.'

"And I said, 'Good. Tell Mr. Biergarten it's urgent, tell him to call me. My name is Sam Goodlow. My number is 396-0161. Please tell him it's a matter of life and death. Tell him to meet me at Sledge's Restaurant, tomorrow, at 8:00 P.M.'

"And Matthew said, 'That's Sledge's, tomorrow, at 8:00. I've got it, Mr. Goodlow. And may I tell him what this is about?'

"And I said, 'Just tell him there's someone I want him to meet. Someone I need identified.'

"And Matthew said, 'Identified. Yes. I see.' And he sneezed.

"I said, 'God bless you,' and he said, 'Thank you.' "

"You've got quite a memory, Sam."

"I was five years old. Five. A long, long time ago. Never. And I was in kindergarten, and there was a little girl I was interested in. Her name was Terry Lee Davis—oh what a cute thing she was, Rye, and I came up to her after school one day and I said to her, 'Hi, my name is Sam. Will you be my girlfriend?' And she giggled the way five-year-old girls do.

"I was eight years old, and I had a cat whose name was Cat. That was my father's idea. Cat. Stupid, I told him. Cat for a cat. He didn't care. He thought he was clever. He wasn't. I didn't want to tell him.

"I was fourteen, I was horny, I was horny, and I was dancing with a girl who was fourteen. Her name was Samantha. Sam and Samantha. I thought it was perfect. I put my hand on her ass while we were dancing. It was a school dance. Ninth Grade Hop. We were all dressed like stiffs. I put my hand on Samantha's ass and she let me keep it there a few seconds. Then she stepped away and looked angry and slapped me.

"I was four years old. It was my birthday. There were my Mom and Dad with their huge smiles because I was four and it was my birthday. As if no one had ever turned four. Only their son.

"I was twenty-six. My father died.

"I was thirteen. Masturbating for the first time. Late bloomer. Finding ecstasy. *I can do this to myself,* I thought.

"Fifteen. Lost in the woods.

"Thirty-one. Broken heart. Oh Leslie, Leslie, what a time it was . . ."

Ryerson listened for a long while without interrupting. He grew sad because he thought that he was hearing a life winding down, was watching a candle going out.

TWENTY-FOUR

The headline on page two of the *Boston Herald* read:

MAN TELLS BIZARRE STORY

Fredrick Barnard, 85, was never a religious man, at least not until three days ago, when, he says, he walked smack dab into and then right through his cellar wall, and found himself in another world.

According to Mr. Barnard, that world is the place that the rest of us refer to as Heaven, The Other Side, The Afterlife, Nirvana. But it is not, Mr. Barnard claims, anything like the place most of us have come to believe in. In some ways, Mr. Barnard says, it is a place of nightmares. But it is also, "a place of great peace and contentment, where we have a chance to experience again, and as often as we like, the happiest moments from our lives here on earth."

His daughter, Hanna Beckford, goes a long way to corroborate his story . . .

"Yes," said Matthew Peters nervously, "I remember. Someone did call." He nodded. "And yes, I remember that his name was Goodlow. If you say that it was *Sam* Goodlow, then that has to be what his name was. He might have said Samuel, but I don't think so."

Ryerson sighed. "For God's sake, Matthew—" He fought back his anger. "Do you remember where you put the damned message, at least?"

Matthew nodded again. "I hope it wasn't very important, Mr. Biergarten."

"It was."

"Oh. I'm sorry." He nodded to indicate a telephone table in the foyer, went over to it, opened the drawer, took out a folded sheet of yellow notepaper, and handed it to Ryerson.

Ryerson unfolded the piece of notepaper and read, "Goodlow. Sledge's. 8:00 P.M., June 5. Important! Need someone identified." He stared at the words for a long while; they were a real, tangible connection between him and the living Sam Goodlow. They seemed more real, in fact, than the spirit of Sam Goodlow himself.

Jenny Goodlow stood in the center of her brother's office and said aloud, "Where are you, Sammy?" The phrasing of the question was very odd, she realized, because she had never, in their adult lives, called her brother "Sammy." It had always been "Sam," except when they were small children. Perhaps that was why she called him "Sammy," now. It made him more childlike—in an odd way, it made him seem more accessible. Perhaps she was calling to the spirit of the child in him, which, she thought, would come to her easily, and enthusiastically.

Sam Goodlow was in a wide, sunlit meadow and he was naked. Around him, honeybees foraged noisily among the wildflowers which grew in a crazy-quilt abundance here.

There were trees all around at the far horizon and he

could see them well—each leaf, and each vein in each leaf, the topography of the bark.

His life was with him in the meadow. He could touch it, smell it, see it—the images were as real as his awareness of them. They danced sensually about him, at once teasing and mocking because they were so temptingly just beyond his grasp.

He felt caressed by these images, and slapped by them, pushed by them, tugged by them. They made him cold and they made him warm. He felt as if he were on a stormy but benevolent ocean, in this meadow, surrounded by the images of his life.

He had evolved since the first moments after the Lincoln Town Car had run him down, since he had come into this new . . . awareness. And he knew that he was evolving, now, that he was changing, that he was becoming something he never was, and had always been.

Sam Goodlow. Stocky and baby faced, the infant beneath the rounded exterior.

That man was dead. Perhaps not physically (that had yet to be proved), but in every other way that mattered.

Here he was, naked and looking very white and out-of-shape in this sunlit meadow.

Then he was no longer in the sunlit meadow.

He was in Ryerson Biergarten's office, and a big man he thought he recognized was there, too, tearing the place apart.

It was just like the old woman not to tell him what the hell he would be looking for, the big man thought. Her and her damned penchant for secrecy.

Penchant, he thought, and smiled. Good word. He had always been good with words.

He threw open a desk drawer that he had already looked into a half-dozen times. The drawer contained a couple of pens, a Swingline stapler, a snapshot of an olive-skinned woman with dark hair, a notepad with complex, geometric doodles in red and green ink around the edges of the pages, but no writing, some paperclips, and a stick of Carefree cinnamon gum. The big man scowled. Same shit he had looked at before. He picked up the stick of gum, unwrapped it, and popped it into his mouth. He scowled again. It was stale.

"What the hell am I looking for?" he whispered.

You'll know when you find it, the old woman had told him cryptically.

"It's a Zen thing," he heard.

"Huh?"

"It's a Zen thing. Don't concentrate on anything, just *do* it!"

The big man glanced quickly around the room. The voice seemed to be omnidirectional. "Where are you?" he demanded.

"I might ask you the same question, my friend."

"What *is* this shit!"

"Wait, wait—I know you. We've never met, it's true, but I do know you."

"Show yourself, goddammit!"

Silence.

"I said show yourself!"

Nothing.

Sam didn't believe that he would always be a kid, and he thought that this was a very adult way for a kid to be thinking.

These years were years he knew he would look back on

later in his life, when he was in his twenties, his thirties, his forties—when his body started falling apart and his life began drawing to a close. These years and these memories would form a kind of exquisite cushion for him as death drew near.

For now, it was wonderful just being a kid, wonderful to be able to run as far and as fast as he wanted, and never tire, wonderful to be able to eat practically anything and not grow fat, wonderful to have all those years *ahead,* to look forward to all the baffling and enchanting experiences that people had as they grew. Love. Career. *Being* whatever it was that he would eventually turn out to be.

He wondered only briefly how he had come to think all this on such a gorgeous day, the kind of day when his young head was usually filled with nothing at all, when his body enjoyed the warm air, and the heady smells of this place, and, if he concentrated on anything, it was only on what shapes the clouds were forming.

"Show yourself," he heard.

He glanced about, through the tall grasses that surrounded him.

"You'll have to find me," he called, hoping that, by calling out, he hadn't given away where he was hiding. If he had, it was okay. When she found him, they would either play more of this kid's game. Or they would play at something else. Something more interesting. And more adult.

"Show yourself, goddammit!" But that wasn't her, Sam realized. It was a man's voice.

He looked at his hands. They were huge. He didn't recognize them. They were the hands of a man.

The tall grasses vanished.

He felt suddenly heavy, and old.

TWENTY-FIVE

In the house where Violet McCartle once lived, there were three attics. One of these attics, the largest, was used as a storage area for collectibles from nearly two centuries—couches, lamps, clocks, tables, armoires, benches, vases, paintings, photographs, a circa 1930 telephone connected to nothing but the air.

The north section of roof in this huge attic needed repair. Under a good, soaking rain, the roof leaked badly; as a result, many of the collectibles stored here were water damaged. A red velvet Queen Anne chair had been ruined. The veneer on a cherry highboy had begun to rise. The works inside a fine old grandfather clock had rusted and the clock was unuseable.

And despite the conscientious efforts of an army of exterminators, there were rats in the attic, too, and they danced on everything, adding their droppings to the mess that the water made.

Some things in the attic, however, were beyond ruination by foraging rats and leaking rainwater.

The woman who called herself Violet McCartle said, "The fact that you found nothing makes no difference. Mr. Bier-

garten will come back here—he has no choice, does he?—
and when he does, then you can do what you so devoutly
want to do to him." She hesitated. "Now tell me about our
upstairs visitor."

"He's no longer a problem," the big man said.

She shook her head. "Wrong. He'll always be a problem.
If he had remained in this house, he would have been a
much larger problem than he now constitutes."

"I understand."

"Of course you do. It's not a terribly difficult concept.
There are some things anyone, no matter how limited, can
understand."

The big man took this as an insult, but said nothing.
Someday, she would simply go too far. As was true with
everyone, her ego would be her undoing.

Sam Goodlow said, "It moves."

Ryerson said, "What moves?"

"The way in."

"The way in to what?"

"And out. It's a moveable place. People go in and out all
the time. They go into their kitchen, they're out. They leave
their kitchen, they're in. They stand on the bathroom scale
and then step off the bathroom scale, they're in and out.
Who knows when or where? And then they disappear sometimes. Hell, hell, they disappear in droves sometimes, like
lemmings off the cliffs of Dover, into the great sea.

"Do you know, do you know, it is only for convenience
sake that death facilitates such things, Ryerson. Who needs
death to do it? Not a soul. *I* didn't, because here I am, whole
and fleshy.

"But there it is. That convenience. Lifeless body, whoosh,

off you go. It's easier, I think it's easier that way than going off whole and fleshy.

"And now, here you go, this place, this person Fredrick and his cat."

Silence.

"And?" Ryerson coaxed.

"I am struck, struck. Ryerson, who can do it but you? This woman married to the asshole is one of you. I am not one of her, I think. It's becoming clear, sometimes it's clear, sometimes not. I want it to be clear. But who can touch her, grasp her, reach in and take her out of there?"

Silence.

"You're going to have to be more specific, Sam."

"Rain, rain go away. These are the times to dry men's souls."

"Sam, you're speaking in riddles again. You're going to have to be more specific."

Nothing.

"Sam, please."

"Mr. Goodlow," Ryerson heard. It was a woman's voice, and he thought that he recognized it. It was the voice of the woman who called herself Violet McCartle.

"Yes?" Ryerson heard. It was Sam's voice.

"I'm concerned about this woman, Mr. Goodlow. And you should be, too. I can't trust her. I'm sure I can't trust her. Come here tomorrow, Mr. Goodlow, and bring some-one who *knows.*"

"Knows what?"

"People. Things. Situations. Someone who will look at her and *know* it is not me. And when he does . . ." The voice drifted quickly into incoherence, and then was gone.

TWENTY-SIX

Ryerson read the article titled MAN TELLS BIZARRE STORY a day after it appeared, and after he read it, he called Hanna Beckford.

"Yes," she said, "I've heard of you, Mr. Biergarten. And I can understand your interest in my father's experience. As a matter of fact, our minister suggested we call you. As luck would have it, you called us first."

"Have you been down into your father's cellar since his return?" Ryerson asked.

"No," answered Hanna Beckford. "And neither has my father. I take it you would like to come here and look into this matter firsthand?"

"I would, yes."

The big man said, "You may be smarter than me, but I'm stronger."

"Smarter *equals* stronger. Throughout history, smart people have gotten stupid people to do their bidding—whether in war, or in business, even in love—"

"You're saying I'm stupid?"

"Only by comparison with me."

"Yeah, well your brains work only when they're inside your skull. Remember that."

She smiled. "That was a very nice choice of words. Congratulations. Now go and fetch my suitcases."

Ryerson approached to within a couple of feet of the cellar wall, stopped, looked back. Hanna Beckford was on the bottom cellar stair, watching, clearly anxious.

Ryerson said, "And he . . . walked right into it, you say?"

She nodded stiffly.

"Then he was gone?"

Another nod. "Yes," she whispered.

Fredrick, explaining that his experience was "not one I wish to repeat," had elected to stay upstairs. He was at the kitchen table; the cellar door was open.

Ryerson looked back at Hanna Beckford, then turned to face the wall again, took a deep breath, and stepped forward. He could reach out and touch the wall if he wanted, now. He frowned. Hanna had told him he would smell salt air, fish, wet earth, but he smelled nothing.

All at once, he felt like a fool. He could see himself seizing the moment and stepping forward, *into* the wall, smashing his face on the concrete.

"Move!" he heard. It was a woman's voice. He didn't recognize it. Hanna Beckford's? he wondered. He turned his head and looked at her. "Did you speak?" he asked.

She shook her head.

"Move!" he heard once more. It was the same voice.

He sighed, turned his head toward the wall again, and stepped forward.

He hit the wall hard. Almost at once, there was laughter all around him.

He turned his head and looked at Hanna Beckford, who was looking openmouthed at him, as if in awe.

He put his hand to his nose, then looked at his fingers; his nose was bleeding. "Dammit!" he whispered. Someone was having a good time at his expense.

He smelled salt air. *Only the blood,* he thought.

"Are you all right, Mr. Biergarten?" Hanna asked.

He nodded once, stone faced, embarrassed, then faced the wall again.

"Smell that?" Hanna asked.

"I smell it," Ryerson answered.

"Salt air," Hanna said. "The ocean." A short pause. "Please be careful, Mr. Biergarten."

"Yes," he whispered.

"Move!" he heard. It was Sam Goodlow's voice. Ryerson looked right, left. Only the cellar. "Move, dammit!" he heard.

He stepped forward.

A strong wind slapped at him.

He heard the rushing noise of waves, and he saw a furious, blue-gray sky above.

TWENTY-SEVEN

S he's there," he heard. "Look, dammit!"

He looked. He saw only the blue-gray sky. He felt suspended in it, and this made him light-headed and afraid.

"Plant your feet!" he heard. It was the same voice—the voice of a woman.

He shook his head. His fear was magnifying his light-headedness. He closed his eyes tightly, as if to shut out what was happening to him.

"Plant your feet, goddammit!" he heard.

"In *what?*" he screamed.

"Idiot! In the earth, in the earth!"

"But where?" He opened his eyes. He saw only a blue-gray sky all around, and he felt a stiff wind slapping at him. He smelled salt air. Wet earth.

"Beneath you, for Christ's sake! You'll drift forever if you don't!" The voice was almost taunting him.

"But how do I *do* that?" he pleaded.

"Pretend you're a bird. Make like a sea gull and *land!* How do I know? Who am *I?*

"Do what you have to do and do it now, or this place will be where you will spend eternity!"

He was not aware of his body, so he supposed, with awe, that he had no control of it. He could see his legs and his arms, and they were in a position that suggested he was walking.

"Am I walking?" he shouted.

"How can you be walking? On what?"

"On the earth!"

"But you aren't *on* the earth."

"How can I . . . Dammit, how can I plant my feet in the earth if I'm not on the earth?"

"It's just an expression. Get your feet on the ground. Get your priorities straight. Get hold of yourself. Know who you are and where you are and what in the hell you're doing!" The voice had changed. It was no longer the voice of a woman. It was a voice he recognized, but could not place.

"I don't know what you're talking about!" he screamed. And now, caught up in his fear and light-headedness, and in the midst of nothing but sky, in the constant wind slapping at him, he knew that he was falling, that he was plummeting at some awful speed toward . . . what? Only God knew, he told himself.

"Wrong," the voice said, *"you* know!"

And at last he recognized the voice. It was his voice. Himself. It was the creature inside him that knew so much more than he knew, the creature that saw the world around it without the limiting effects of the senses feeding impulses to the brain, which changed those impulses into something plausible and recognizable.

This all around him—the furious, blue-gray sky and wind and salt air—were only the products of his brain and senses trying in vain to cope with what was *real,* what that creature inside him could see and feel without sight, or touch.

"Not so smart, after all, huh?" the voice taunted.

"You're right," Ryerson admitted.

And the voice finished, "It's really pretty much of a Zen thing, Rye."

Ryerson cracked a nervous grin, closed his eyes, opened them.

He saw what looked for all the world like clay all around him—red clay, green clay, black clay, orange, pink, mauve, gray. There were endless mounds of it, like multicolored hills, and they stretched beyond his sight.

"What in the hell is *this?*" he whispered.

"Only what it looks like," he heard. "More or less. The stuff of dreams and memories. They have to be rebuilt from *something*. This is that something."

"I don't believe it."

"So noted."

"But it's impossible—"

"It is the stuff of the universe."

He bent over, fingered some of it. It was much like the dirt floor in Jack Lutz's cabin, where Stevie had disappeared. It was moist, almost fluid. But it was also incredibly malleable. With quick, deft movements of his figners— much quicker and more deft than they had ever been before—he fashioned first a perfect cube with the stuff, then a sphere, then the miniature likeness of Creosote.

The likeness cocked its head at him, wheezed, gurgled. Ryerson stood up quickly, surprised; the likeness fell from his hand and instantly became again a part of the stuff it had sprung from.

Ryerson heard, "It's full of protein, you know. It needs to be. But don't eat it." Laughter.

Ryerson glanced about.

Stevie Lutz was within arm's reach, her gaze outward, beyond him, lost.

"Mrs. Lutz?" he said.

He got no response.

He reached, got hold of her hand, tugged.

"No!" she screamed. "Let me be!" And her gaze leveled on him.

"My God," he whispered. She *wanted* to stay here, had wanted to come here in the first place. "Mrs. Lutz," he shouted, "come with me. Please." And he pulled hard.

But she slipped away, ran off, and was absorbed.

And, at once, Ryerson found himself again in Hanna Beckford's cellar, and she was looking openmouthed at him, the same way she had when he had walked into the cement wall and bloodied his nose.

The note from Matthew Peters was taped on a mirror above the telephone stand. "Call Captain Willis. Urgent."

Ryerson called.

"Rye," Willis said, "I thought you should know; this woman, Violet McCartle—Big Mama, remember—was found dead in some woods just outside Boston."

"How long had she been dead, Bill?"

"The coroner's not certain, but he says at least ten days, perhaps longer."

"Thanks. I'll get back to you."

He hung up, went out to the Woody, and started driving to Violet McCartle's home.

From the backseat, Sam Goodlow said, "You're leaving her there?"

Ryerson lurched. Sam had startled him. He glanced in the rearview mirror and saw him as a patchwork of pink skin, eyebrows, hair, eyes, nose, as if he were made from errant bits of fabric. "Leaving who where?"

"The asshole's wife," Sam answered. "Are you leaving her there? In that place she's in."

Ryerson felt as if he'd been put on the spot. He squirmed, didn't know how to answer.

"Lily liver," Sam said.

Ryerson glanced at him again, then at the road. "You're right, Sam."

"Of course I am. What do you want? I *know.*" He made a shivering noise. "Jesus. Someone danced on my grave. That happens all the time, now."

Ryerson came to a stopsign, looked quickly right and left, saw nothing, started into the intersection.

"Gnats!" Sam screamed, and Ryerson hit the brake pedal hard. "Gnats!" Sam screamed again.

Ryerson turned his head and looked at Sam, who seemed terrified. "I hate them. Gnats. Everywhere."

"What are you talking about? Gnats?"

"Gnats? Who said gnats?"

"You did."

"I did? Who knows what I say or what I mean? And when I die, they'll be all over me, I think—"

"Sam, you *are* dead!"

Sam looked blankly at him a moment. "Am I? Really? Can you prove it?"

"Sam, we've been over this before."

"We have? I don't remember."

A horn sounded. Sam said, "Get a move on there, you're holding up traffic."

The big man at the gate to Violet McCartle's house remembered Ryerson. He said, "I'm sorry, Mr. Biergarten, but I have orders to keep you from entering." He grinned strangely. "Unless, of course, you have a compelling reason. *Do* you have a compelling reason, Mr. Biergarten?"

"As compelling as they come, my friend. Perhaps you could simply tell Mrs. McCartle that I have information she'll find quite useful."

"Don't we all," said the big man. He was still grinning strangely, and Ryerson easily read violence in it.

Ryerson said, "And I'm sure the police will find the information I have useful, too."

The big man's grin did not alter. "I must warn you, Mr. Biergarten, that if I let you into this estate, you will find it very hard indeed to leave."

"That's a chance I'll have to take," Ryerson said.

"Suit yourself," the big man said, and he went and called the house. Moments later, the gates opened, and Ryerson drove through.

As she had on their first visit, the woman who called herself Violet McCartle greeted Ryerson at the top of the long flight of steps. She was smiling cordially, but Ryerson read from her the same sort of malice and violence that he had read from the man at the gate. He glanced quickly about; there was no sign of Sam Goodlow.

"Won't you come in, Mr. Biergarten," the woman said, and gestured toward the open door behind her.

Ryerson followed her inside.

They went into the same expansive living room, crowded with rococo furnishings, that they had used before. Ryerson sat on a white rococo couch. The woman who called herself Violet McCartle sat nearby, on a green settee. Sunlight— seldom seen in the past two weeks—coming in through a pair of large windows in front of her made the woman's face look unnaturally white and smooth.

She said, "My man told me you had some information I might find useful." She smiled, again cordially, invitingly.

Ryerson nodded and smiled back. He felt like he was playing a game with the woman, and he wasn't sure that this was wise. "I thought you should know that a woman named Violet McCartle was found dead yesterday."

The woman's cordial smile did not slip as she said, "Mr. Biergarten, you realize of course that you have done a very, very foolish thing coming here? I think my man actually told you that what you were doing was unwise, isn't that right?"

Ryerson nodded and tried, unsuccessfully, to keep his smile from faltering. "Perhaps you could tell me who you are."

"That turns out to be a philosophical question, Mr. Biergarten. If Violet McCartle no longer exists, and if I appear to *be* her, and if I act for her in her business dealings—as I was hired to do—and if everyone I deal with *believes* that I am Violet McCartle, then that is indeed who I am. We are judged by the world around us, so for all intents and purposes—all that matter, at any rate—I am the person I was hired to be. And if, at one time, I was known by some other name, then that woman no longer exists either. The philosophical and *physical* conundrum is satisfied."

"That's bullshit," Ryerson said. "And it's not even *good* bullshit."

"Quite," the woman said, and stopped smiling abruptly. "I am not a kind or generous person, Mr. Biergarten. *You* of all people should have sensed that."

"I did."

"And yet you have come here—"

"There are people who know I'm here."

She waved this announcement away. "Oh, Mr. Biergarten, do you think that that is of any significance to me? It isn't. I'm not going to be staying here for long. A half hour, at most. Then I'm gone, and I assure you that no one is going to be able to find me. Money can accomplish miracles, Mr. Biergarten." She paused. Her smile reappeared, but it was grim. "You, however, are going to be staying here, in this house, just as your friend Mr. Goodlow has."

TWENTY-EIGHT

Ryerson sensed someone behind him. He turned his head, looked. The big man who had been tending the gate stood ten feet away. The man nodded and said, "I did warn you, Mr. Biergarten."

"So you did," Ryerson said.

He thought that he could run. He'd done a fair amount of running in college, and had been jogging for ten years. He was in good shape and certainly could outsprint the man behind him, who was clearly built more for strength than speed.

The man withdrew a revolver from his jacket pocket and leveled it at Ryerson's head.

Ryerson attempted a smile and said to the woman, "Perhaps you could tell me why you had Sam Goodlow killed."

The woman did not smile back. She grimaced, as if in annoyance. "Oh, my dear Mr. Biergarten, do you think this is some made-for-TV movie, and all the answers are going to be given to you before the villain does you in?" She shook her head. "It doesn't work that way. I'm sorry. Even if I did answer your question, it wouldn't do you, or me, or my man there any good whatever."

Ryerson shrugged. "I simply thought—"

"Photographs," the woman cut in smilingly. "A damning pair of photographs of me and the woman I have since become. Your friend, Mr. Goodlow, had possession of these photographs, and now I do. He became something of a complication, which is why he was killed." Her smile faded. "And I'm afraid, sir, that that is all I'm going to say." She nodded at the big man, then stood, and stepped away.

Ryerson knew why she had stepped away—she was getting out of the big man's line of fire.

Ryerson rolled forward, off the rococo couch, heard the clap of the revolver going off, and felt a millisecond of intense pain at the back of his head.

Rats are true omnivores. They will eat whatever is available, and their digestive systems are fully capable of handling anything they can chew and swallow.

They are scavengers as well as predators and will attack creatures many times their size. They are as fearless as badgers, as stealthy as cats, nearly as intelligent as dogs, as adaptive and resilient as human beings themselves, and they are found in virtually every country on earth.

Several families of rats lived a contented existence in the three attics in the house that had belonged to the late Violet McCartle. The place they had claimed as their own was warm, relatively dry—except in the largest attic space—and food was plentiful. Squirrels often made the mistake of coming into the attic spaces from one of the large oak and willow trees that crowded the house, and when a squirrel did show up, a half dozen of the rats—which had grown large and fat from their carefree lifestyle—cornered the hapless creature and tore it apart.

The body that was dressed in a gray suit lay on its back.

The suit was wet because the roof leaked badly and rain in the last seven days had been nearly continuous.

The body was only a pale shadow of what it had been barely two weeks earlier. The rats had gone first for its substantial gut, then the eyes and the genitals, and were now working their way contentedly and noisily through what remained.

Ryerson Biergarten lay on his stomach beside the body. Several rats were already tentatively sniffing around Ryerson's feet and hands, and they liked what they smelled.

Sam Goodlow thought he recognized the body in the gray suit. It was certainly not much of a body, he thought. It lacked . . . definition. Mass. Stature. It looked like a chunky inflatable doll that had lost air in strange places.

He bent over, reached out, and touched the body at the shoulder. He felt nothing for a moment.

Then his arm tingled and he realized that it had not tingled that way—had not felt *alive*—for quite some time, and he thought it was proof of what he had been telling Ryerson Biergarten this past week. He wasn't dead! How could he be dead and have a tingling arm?

His arm stopped tingling.

The big attic space vanished.

Another space took its place.

It was a large, white space, harshly lit, and it had lots of reflective surfaces. He smelled antiseptic and blood.

And there was a face. A mask covered the mouth. Big, horn-rimmed glasses. These words came from the mouth beneath the mask: "That's good, Mrs. Goodlow, there he is—"

Sam lurched back from the body. The big, dimly lit attic space returned at once.

And he thought, *I recognize the body in the gray suit.*

He grew afraid. He had never before in his life been so very afraid.

Stevie Lutz was afraid, too.

This man standing so close by was the same man who had caught hold of her and had tried to pull her from this place, and he was going to try and do that again. She knew it. He had that look about him. That look of resolve and tenacity.

That pity.

Damn him! She had no need of his pity.

"Go away!" she screamed.

He held his hand out to her.

"No. I don't *want* to go back!" she screamed.

"But you have a life to live," he told her.

She laughed. "A *life* to live? You've got to be kidding. My life is a joke."

"And what do you have here?"

She looked him in the eye. "Life here is what *I* make of it." She smiled as if to say she knew something he didn't, and added, "Literally."

"And how is that so terribly different from the other life you have?"

She stared at him a moment, then said, "I am *controlled* there. *He* controls me"—meaning Jack Lutz—"our *circumstances* control me, my expectations control me."

"And nothing controls you here?"

"Nothing at all."

"Except them."

"Them? Who?"

"Them." He nodded.

Stevie turned, looked behind her, and screamed.

* * *

Sam Goodlow touched the body in the gray suit at the feet. His arm tingled, and the big, dimly lit attic space vanished. He was in bed.

Rebecca Meechum was with him, and she was grinning. He had never before seen such a grin from her. It was sad and evil at the same time, as if she were trying to share a pain that she adored.

Sam stepped back from the body in the gray suit. Rebecca Meechum vanished.

The big, dimly lit attic space reappeared.

The body of the man in the gray suit reappeared.

The other body reappeared.

Sam looked at it. He saw the blood at the temple, and he reached out to touch the body. His finger went into it. He recoiled.

This was Ryerson Biergarten.

Only faces can show real hunger, fear, pain, loneliness. Eyes become hollow, dark, and ironically large and lifeless at the same time. Mouths hang open. Skin tightens over the bone. There is no movement in such faces. They are as motionless as stone. But they are unlike stone because clearly there is a skull beneath, and a brain inside the skull, and a scream inside the brain. That scream is silent and deafening and endless.

It's what Stevie Lutz heard from the faces she looked at.

"They control you! *They* use you!" the man with her shouted.

And she went forward at once, took the man's hand.

And when she touched him, he vanished.

The world she inhabited vanished.

She found herself once again inside the hunter's cabin.

She left the cabin quickly and started for home.

She would deal with Jack. *She* was in control now!

Sam Goodlow thought, looking at the body which lay on its stomach next to his body, *This is my friend.*

Because friends shared the truth.

And the truth, he realized at last, was undeniable. The body in the gray suit was him. *Had* been him.

Now it was rat food.

And it was time for him—the *real* Sam Goodlow—to move on to better things.

To other things, anyway.

Different things.

He felt confused. What sort of things was he supposed to move on to? He had no idea. He felt stuck. He realized that he *had* felt stuck ever since . . . He stared at the body in the gray suit. Ever since *this.*

He sighed. "Where," he whispered, "do I go from here?"

He heard, from just behind him, "Let me show you."

He looked. Ryerson Biergarten stood close by.

Sam jumped back, surprised.

"It's all right," Ryerson said.

Sam shook his head. "No, it isn't. You're not dead, Rye."

"Sure I am." He nodded at his body lying on its stomach next to the body in the gray suit. "See there. It's obvious, Sam. You're still in a kind of strange denial—"

"Oh, shit, Rye, *I* ought to know what dead is. And you're not dead."

Ryerson looked suddenly baffled, and a little sad. "But, Sam . . . there I am." He indicated the body on the floor.

Sam looked at the body for a couple of moments. He

sighed. "What do I know, Rye. Maybe I'm just being a jerk. Maybe you really are dead."

Ryerson smiled oddly. "And if I am—well, it's obvious that I am, isn't it?—then it's not a bad thing. Look at what I've been all my life, Sam—I've been someone who pokes his nose around in the paranormal. Hell, now I *am* the paranormal. Now I can poke my nose around in earnest—" His cheek twitched.

Sam said, "You've got a little tic there."

"I noticed," Ryerson said.

Sam put himself in a velvet Queen Anne chair near his body. He slouched in the chair, his big hands flat on the arms, and his legs out straight, so they were near the top of what had once been his head. He said, "It's good knowing just who you are, Rye. And exactly *what* you are."

"That's very profound, Sam."

"I can't help but be profound in the state I'm in."

"I imagine not." His cheek twitched again and he tried to ignore it.

He sat cross-legged on the floor near his own body. A rat was sniffing around his body's neck and he said, nodding at it, "Look there, Sam, a rat's sniffing around my neck." He was trying to sound casual and offhanded.

"That's disgusting," Sam said.

"No, no," Ryerson protested. "It isn't disgusting. It's *life*. Really. We all survive off death, in one way or another. Sweep out the old, sweep in the new—" He smiled. His cheek twitched again. "I mean, Sam, look at what the rats have done to you there. There's hardly anything left; is *that* disgusting?"

Sam thought about this a moment, then shook his head. "No. I suppose I see what you mean."

"Of course you do. It's the soul of good sense. Why

should what's natural and . . . beautiful for *you* be disgusting for *me?* That's kind of inequitable, wouldn't you say?" Another rat appeared and sniffed around Ryerson's knee. His stomach felt queasy, and he thought this was odd. Why should his stomach feel queasy when he really didn't *have* a stomach any more? "Now look there," he said, and attempted to smile again, but it worked badly, "another one. Soon, all the . . . physicalness that was me will be gone, and that will be a good thing—"

"You're being an asshole," Sam said.

Ryerson gave him a surprised look.

A shot rang out from below.

Both men snapped their gaze in the direction of the floor.

Another shot rang out.

"I know what's happening," Sam said.

"Yes," Ryerson said.

"She's killing him."

"Yes. It's clear."

"The goon. She's killing him. I knew she'd do it. She's not a kind person, Rye. She does terrible things."

Another shot.

"He takes a lot of killing, I guess," Ryerson said.

"A big man," Sam said. "Not a terribly evil man, either. But evil enough. She's wise, I suppose, to kill him. He would simply have done it to her before long."

"You're talking very clearly," Ryerson said.

"I'm clear on a lot of things now, Rye. I want to thank you for that."

Another shot. And another.

"She's making sure," Sam said.

"Thank me for what?" Ryerson asked.

"For making things clear. For bringing me to this place. To him." He nodded to indicate the body in the gray suit.

They heard a strange *whumping* noise from below.

"Shot?" Ryerson asked.

"I don't know," Sam said. "I don't think so. It didn't sound like a shot. It sounded like someone being hit in the head. I think it was someone being hit in the head."

"Him?" Ryerson asked.

Sam nodded. "Of course. Who else? It was him."

"How do you know?"

"I know a lot. Things are very clear now."

"For instance?"

Sam sat forward in the Queen Anne chair, so his legs were bent and his elbows were on his knees. He conjured up a thoughtful look. "For instance, like the fact that we heard her fire the last shot. It was six shots, so it was the last shot."

Ryerson shook his head. "Some automatics fire more than six shots, Sam. Some of them fire . . . a lot more. Twelve, I think. I'm surprised you don't know that." His cheek twitched once, then, very quickly, again.

"You have a little twitch there, Rye."

"I noticed."

"And like the fact that that woman is on her way up here now to check us out."

"You're kidding."

Sam grinned. "I wouldn't kid you, Rye. Not now."

They both heard the sound of a door opening from below.

"That's her," Sam said.

They heard a moan.

"What was that?" Ryerson said, surprised.

"You," Sam said.

"I didn't moan. It wasn't me."

Sam nodded at the body lying at Ryerson's feet. "It was him. It was you."

"It couldn't have been him. He's dead. And I'm going to go on an oddyssey of discovery in the great . . ." He faltered.

"Beyond?" Sam offered.

"Yes. The Great Beyond."

"Asshole!"

Ryerson looked offended. "Why do you call me an asshole? That hardly seems kind."

Sam shrugged. "I stopped being kind, simply for the sake of it, three weeks ago."

"Meaning?"

"Meaning, what you did for the other asshole's wife you can sure as hell do for yourself."

"I don't understand."

"Of course you do. You're being thickheaded because you think you're dead and so it's time to have some fun. Well, you *aren't* dead, Rye, and if you were, I'm here to tell you that it simply isn't a lot of fun."

Another moan.

Then the sound of footsteps from the farthest of the three attics.

Sam said, "You know what she's going to do. She's going to put a bullet in your head, just to be sure."

"I thought she was out of bullets."

"Idiot! She reloaded. And she's really looking forward to pumping your head up and splattering your brains all over the place. She'll even overlook her fear of rats, and the smell of that!"—he nodded to indicate the body in the gray suit. "She's on a roll, Ryerson. She's really full of herself, and she's aiming to leave this place without any messy loose ends."

"Which," Ryerson offered, "is what you were, I think. A loose end. And that's why she had you killed."

Sam nodded ruefully. "A loose end. Yes. It does wonders for the ego."

"And I don't know why you think," Ryerson went on, "that the idea of her shooting that . . . thing"—he nodded at the body at his feet—"should bother me, Sam. If I really *were* alive—"

"This isn't macho time in the great hereafter, Rye. My God, talk about denial. For the past week, *you've* been trying to convince *me* that I was dead. Well, thank you, you've done it. Now it's my turn." He leaned way forward in the chair, impossibly forward in the chair, so his back was yards longer than it should have been, and his head became as big as a pumpkin, and he screamed, "Ryerson Biergarten, you're alive! *Alive!* You're still breathing, still sweating, still digesting, still able to make love, still able to dream, and pee, and eat ice cream, still able to go for Sunday drives, and have your heart broken, and your knee-caps busted, and your hair cut, and your contracts renewed. *Alive,* my friend! So do yourself a favor and *act* like you're alive before she turns *you* into rat chow."

Ryerson stared at the huge face that was so close to his and his cheek twitched again.

TWENTY-NINE

The woman who called herself Violet McCartle felt pumped. She felt strong, powerful, invincible. She felt that she could unload the .38 she carried into her own brain and it would do her no harm whatever.

Even the idea of coming up here, into the midst of this corruption and decay, was undaunting. A powerful, invincible person simply did what was necessary, even if it was distasteful.

She could see past the triangular entryways through the first and second attic spaces, and into the largest attic, the third, though not clearly. She could see that a light was on in the third attic, and it dimly illuminated the two centuries worth of collectibles stored there.

She could also hear the raucous and joyful squeals of the rats.

And she could smell the dead man. She thought, in fact, that she could smell him *too* well, as if her sense of smell had suddenly increased ten-thousand-fold.

But she knew that she was smiling through it all because the bottom line was simple—she was a superior human being. She had bested Violet McCartle, who had assumed, so stupidly, that because they looked so much alike, their psyches and their souls were identical, too. Then she had gone on to eliminate all those who could stand in her way, and now could count herself as one of the very wealthy. And wealth equalled power. And power equalled control.

She would no longer be controlled by those around her. She would be the one in control, she would be the one to decide who did what, and to whom, and why.

Wasn't that, after all, the right and privilege of a superior human being? To control. To wield power over the inferior, who could not know what was good for them, anyway.

And those who betrayed her—like the big man, who had persisted in his transparent lies even when he had to have known that *she* knew he was lying (and who so often made his idiotic threats to scatter her brains about)—would fall victim to her withering and merciless judgment, as would those who opposed her, and those who could oppose her, and those who supported them, and those, like Rebecca Meechum and Sam Goodlow, who were simply too stupid to go on living, and those, like Ryerson Biergarten, who were too damned smart for their own good, and those—

She heard a moan. It seemed very loud. Too loud.

The side of her head hurt and she didn't know why. She touched it, felt it, sensed her fingers moving in, through her temple. She withdrew her hand, looked at it, saw a mass of coagulated blood. But then it was gone, and she moved forward.

She was at the entrance to the second attic space and she peered through it, into the third attic. She called, "Mr. Biergarten, it seems you are in pain. I am here to relieve it." And she chuckled.

Sam Goodlow said, "She's a funny woman."

Ryerson could say nothing. He was watching himself breathe and listening to himself moan.

Sam stood. "You're very quiet suddenly," he said. He went over to the circa 1930 phone, picked it up, dialed it.

Ryerson looked at him. "You can't call anyone on that thing," he said. "It's not hooked up."

"Neither am I," Sam said. Then, speaking into the telephone, "Captain Willis, please."

The woman who called herself Violet McCartle did not want to believe that she heard talking from within the third attic, but she knew that she did, and it troubled her. If Ryerson Biergarten were talking to himself, it meant either that he was delirious, or that he was crazy. If he was crazy, then he would pose the particular kind of threat that crazy people posed—he would be unpredictable. And unpredictable people were always in control because other people didn't know what the hell they were going to do, and so everyone was afraid of them. And if power equalled control, so did fear.

But it was really no problem at all, she decided. A bullet in the brain would cure his unpredictability, and his craziness, in a microsecond.

"Mr. Biergarten," she said, as she advanced through the all-but-empty second attic, "if you're crazy, then I have a cure for that, as well." And she chuckled again.

Her head hurt. She put her hand to it, touched, felt, probed, withdrew her hand, saw a pancake-sized mass of deep red tissue. It vanished.

She moved forward.

"Never mind who this is," Sam Goodlow said angrily into the telephone. "Suffice it to say that Captain Willis and I have a mutual friend, Ryerson Biergarten, and he's in a shitload of trouble."

At that moment, Ryerson was tentatively probing at his body with the toe of his shoe, and he was becoming very troubled because his shoe seemed too real—it met resistance when it touched his body, and he had hoped that he could simply slip back in. "I don't understand," he complained. "If I'm here"—he slapped his chest—"in spirit, and there"—he pointed at the body on the floor—"in reality, why the hell can't I—"

"In a moment, Rye," Sam cut in. "They're getting Captain Willis for me."

Ryerson looked at him, astonished. "I need your help here, Sam."

"And you're getting it." He glanced quickly and questioningly toward the second attic, and cocked his head in confusion. Something was very wrong with the woman approaching.

He said into the telephone, "Captain Willis?"

The woman who called herself Violet McCartle looked at her free hand. The fingers of both her hands felt oddly heavy. As if there were fishing sinkers attached. How strange. She couldn't remember having had such a feeling before. Perhaps it was simply the weight of the pistol. Six pounds of metal was certainly a heavy weight for anyone to carry at the end of an outstretched arm.

But her toes felt heavy, too, she noticed. A circulatory problem, perhaps. If extremities could tingle and fall asleep because of circulatory problems, then it was certainly possible for them to feel heavy.

But, no matter, she decided.

She still felt pumped, powerful, invincible. And she had a chore to dispense with.

"Mr. Biergarten," she called through the second attic, "your days as a sentient being have come to an end."

Sam Goodlow said into the telephone, "But this really is Sam Goodlow."

The toe of Ryerson's shoe penetrated an inch or so into his thigh. He smiled. He was getting somewhere.

Sam Goodlow said into the telephone, "I'm not a woman. I'm a man. Why the hell would you think you're talking to a woman?"

Ryerson looked at him. "Trouble?"

Sam held the phone out, clearly astonished. "He hung up on me. The bastard hung up on me. He thought I was a woman. I'm not a woman! Do I *sound* like a woman?"

Ryerson nodded. "Sometimes."

"You're kidding."

Ryerson inclined his chin to indicate his foot, which seemed to be stuck in his thigh. "Can you give me a hand here, Sam. I seem to be having some difficulty."

"When do I sound like a woman?" Sam asked, obviously offended. "I mean, I know I don't possess actual, physical vocal cords any more, so my voice probably comes out kind of—" He glanced suddenly toward the second attic. "Uh-oh!" he said.

Ryerson looked.

The woman who called herself Violet McCartle stood ten feet away, and she was pointing a gun at the body lying on its stomach on the floor—Ryerson's body. She wore a contented grin. She looked as if she were about to eat a chocolate sundae.

"Uh-oh, what?" Ryerson said, because, at that moment, he did not see the woman. He looked again at his foot, which was caught in his thigh.

Sam glanced quickly at Ryerson, then at the woman again, then at Ryerson. "Uh-oh, her!"

The woman who called herself Violet McCartle thought, *What a moment this is. What power at my command. Just a twitch of the finger and a life is extinguished forever.* Which was how long, her thoughts continued, that a moment like this—this moment of godlike control and power—should rightfully be savored. Forever!

Sam looked at the woman. She was in exactly the same position she'd been in ten seconds earlier. Straight arm, gun held tightly, body erect, chocolate-sundae grin.

He looked once more at Ryerson. "You don't see her, do you?"

But then Ryerson did see her. Then she wavered, and was gone. Then she returned, wavered, returned.

Sam said, "She got what was promised her."

Ryerson's foot sank deeper into his thigh, which made his heart pump fast. Christ, this was probably a lot like being born.

"Take it slow," Sam warned.

"Slow, hell!" Ryerson shouted, and his foot flowed into his leg, and his leg followed, and foot and leg were one, and then he felt a headache he knew would last for a very long time.

THIRTY

TWO DAYS LATER

From his hospital bed, Ryerson Biergarten said to Jenny Goodlow, "I know how you feel." He hesitated. "I came to view your brother as a kind of . . . absent friend during the two weeks I was looking for him, and, without meaning to sound presumptuous, I have to say that I feel his loss, too—"

"But I don't understand why they had to kill him, Mr. Biergarten," Jenny cut in.

Ryerson nodded, acknowledging her confusion. "Yes," he said, "I understand that." He hesitated, uncertain how to continue. Sam had died so needlessly, and no one wants to hear that a loved one has died needlessly, at the whim of another. "The real Violet McCartle," Ryerson continued, "was very ill and didn't want her business associates to know. She thought it made her vulnerable in their eyes. So she hired the imposter to take her place in matters of business. She wanted to look hale and hearty, even though she was often confined to a wheelchair. But the woman she hired saw the whole thing as a wonderful opportunity to become the new Violet McCartle. She had Violet killed, and then proceeded to ransack the woman's holdings—her stock portfolio, her bank accounts, et cetera. But before Violet was killed, she hired your brother to take charge of a couple of photographs which showed both her and the imposter together. I believe that Sam became confused, Jenny; I believe that he himself didn't know which woman was the real Violet McCartle, and that's why he called me. He thought I would simply *know* which was the real one. And I think that I would have. But then, Sam was killed." Ryerson paused. "There is some justice in the whole matter. The imposter herself was killed by the man who was supposed to have been her bodyguard." He did not give her the grim details of the woman's death, did not tell her that the woman's perverse spirit had climbed the stairs to the attic, and was there even now, caught forever in her moment of greatest happiness—the moment just before she thought she would pull the trigger and put a bullet in Ryerson's brain.

Jenny Goodlow looked misty eyed. "Sam was such a gentle soul, Mr. Biergarten. I remember that once he caught this little mouse that was living in his office, and he took it out to the park and let it go. Who cares about mice? Only gentle people. And simply looking at him, you probably wouldn't have thought he'd do such a thing. He didn't actually *look* gentle, not unless you really knew him. Or unless you really looked into his eyes. I think he always thought of himself as kind of . . . oafish, I guess. Kind of big and clumsy and oafish. But he was in reality such an exquisitely gentle soul."

Ryerson nodded. "And still is," he said. "And still is."